# Emily Dickinson

**Mitchell Lane PUBLISHERS**

P.O. Box 196
Hockessin, Delaware 19707

# *Poets and Playwrights*

Carl Sandburg

Emily Dickinson

Langston Hughes

Tennessee Williams

William Shakespeare

# Emily Dickinson

Michèle Griskey

Copyright © 2007 by Mitchell Lane Publishers, Inc. All rights reserved. No part of this book may be reproduced without written permission from the publisher. Printed and bound in the United States of America.

Printing     1     2     3     4     5     6     7     8     9

Library of Congress Cataloging-in-Publication Data
Griskey, Michèle.
　Emily Dickinson / by Michele Griskey.
　　p. cm. — (Poets and playwrights)
　Includes bibliographical references and index.
　ISBN 1-58415-429-2 (library bound: alk. paper)
　1. Dickinson, Emily, 1830–1886—Juvenile literature. 2. Poets, American—19th century—Biography—Juvenile literature. I. Title. II. Series.
PS1541.Z5G75 2007
811'.4—dc22
　　　　　　　　　　　　　　　　　　　　　　　　　　　　　　　　　2006006105
ISBN-13: 9781584154297

**ABOUT THE AUTHOR:** Michèle Griskey has a BA in journalism and an MA in English. She teaches writing, research, and philosophy for the University of Phoenix Online. She has written several biographies for Mitchell Lane Publishers, including *Harriet Beecher Stowe*, *Ray Bradbury*, and *Beverly Cleary*. When she was in junior high school, Michèle first read and fell in love with Emily Dickinson's poetry. Since then, Michèle is still inspired by Dickinson's imaginative poetry and mysterious life. Michèle also writes fiction for middle grade and teen readers. She lives on an island in Washington's Puget Sound with her family.

**PHOTO CREDITS:** Cover, pp. 1, 3, 6, 19, 34, 44, 54, 62, 82—Todd-Bingham Picture Collection, Manuscripts and Archives, Yale University Library; p. 9—AP Photo/The Daily Hampshire Gazette, Carol Lollis; p. 14—New York Public Library; p. 24—Houghton Library/Harvard University; p. 27, 29, 36, 76—Library of Congress; p. 64—The Amherst Historical Society; p. 66—Christie's, London; p. 69—University of Massachusetts, Amherst/Special Collections and University Archives; p. 90—Barbara Marvis.

**PUBLISHER'S NOTE:** This story is based on the author's extensive research, which she believes to be accurate. Documentation of such research is contained on page 104.
　The internet sites referenced herein were active as of the publication date. Due to the fleeting nature of some web sites, we cannot guarantee they will all be active when you are reading this book.

PLB

# Contents

| | | |
|---|---|---|
| Chapter 1 | In a House in Amherst | 7 |
| | *FYI: What Is Poetry? | 11 |
| Chapter 2 | Growing Up with Life and Death | 15 |
| | FYI: Tuberculosis | 21 |
| Chapter 3 | Studying Nature | 25 |
| | FYI: Footprints of the Past | 31 |
| Chapter 4 | Away from Home and Back Again | 35 |
| | FYI: American Transcendentalism | 41 |
| Chapter 5 | Emily the Poet | 45 |
| | FYI: The Railroad | 51 |
| Chapter 6 | The Literary Life | 55 |
| | FYI: Emily's Mentor | 61 |
| Chapter 7 | Challenges | 65 |
| | FYI: Cottage Gardens | 71 |
| Chapter 8 | Hiding Away | 75 |
| | FYI: Helen Hunt Jackson | 79 |
| Chapter 9 | Endings | 83 |
| | FYI: The Brontë Sisters | 87 |
| Chapter 10 | The Legacy | 91 |
| | FYI: Emily on eBay | 95 |

| | |
|---|---|
| Chronology | 98 |
| Selected Works | 99 |
| Timeline in History | 100 |
| Chapter Notes | 101 |
| Further Reading | 104 |
|     Works Consulted | 104 |
|     On the Internet | 106 |
| Glossary | 107 |
| Index | 109 |

*For Your Information

The Homestead, where Emily Dickinson lived for most of her life. It was built by Emily's grandfather, Samuel Fowler Dickinson, in 1813.

# Chapter 1

## In a House in Amherst

After the morning chores were done and the bread was set to rise, Emily Dickinson stole away upstairs to her narrow bedroom on the second floor of her family's house. Near the wood post bed, neatly made with a cream-colored cover, she sat down at her little desk. Carefully, she opened the drawer, pulled out a small book of paper that she had stitched together, and placed it on her desk.

Through the open window, Emily could hear the birds singing. Earlier she had been out in the garden. The roses and honeysuckle surrounding the arbor buzzed with bees, and the lilies danced in the breeze. Emily thought of the colorful flowers and felt joy. What a wonderful time of year!

Next door was the impressive house of her brother, Austin, and sister-in-law, Susan. Austin shared many interests with Emily and encouraged her to expand her mind with books. Emily admired and loved Sue dearly. The previous night Sue and Austin had thrown another one of their extravagant parties. Sue was well known for hosting festive events. She would dress in luxurious gowns and entertain noteworthy guests such as Ralph Waldo Emerson, an essayist and a predominant figure in the transcendentalist movement; Bret Harte, a writer well known for depicting life in California; and Frances Hodgson Burnett,

# Chapter 1

who wrote the children's classics *A Little Princess* and *The Secret Garden*. Emily Dickinson had pictured the food and heard the laughter and music in her mind, but she didn't go. It had been years since she had attended such festivities.

At one time she had. Emily had spent many pleasant hours in Austin and Sue's parlor in the company of others. She had shared her wit and improvised unusual songs on the piano . . . but those days were over. Now, only the memories remained.

Out in front of her stately brick house, the bustle of village life in Amherst, Massachusetts, went on. Emily could see it if she looked out her window. Perhaps another lecture about geology would be given at Amherst College. Perhaps a sermon would be given at the Congregational Church.

It was a time of change. Writers and philosophers were defining new ideas and creating a uniquely American literature. The railroad was bringing people to and fro. This extraordinary technology fascinated Dickinson, but it had been many years since she had been on a train. The Civil War had been fought and the United States had been transformed—the slaves were all free. Now women were working on gaining their rights, including the right to vote. Yet to Dickinson, the world outside her house and garden could have been in another galaxy, for she stayed indoors or in the enclosed space of her garden, protected.

Many of the Amherst citizens talked about the once lively woman who now dressed only in white and wouldn't see anyone outside her family. She didn't even attend church anymore. When people asked her to come visit, they received a polite written excuse. Those who made it into her house only heard her soft voice from shadows. Dickinson would speak but would not be seen. On the other hand, the few people to whom she did reach out received passionate letters, a bright bouquet of flowers from her garden, or a strange and touching poem.

Many rumors circulated about Dickinson's isolation. Some thought a broken heart had sent her into exile. Others thought she was afraid

## In a House in Amherst

Emily spent many hours in her bedroom composing poems. A picture of her sister, Lavinia, sits near her bed.

of being around people, that something violent had happened to make her afraid. Some even thought she was insane. What really happened to Emily Dickinson to make her retreat? Even her family wouldn't reveal her reasons.

While Dickinson had become a very private person, her life was far from boring. Her mind raced with thoughts, possibilities, and emotion. She may have been in one geographical area, but her mind seemed to have traveled all over the world. She filled the small space of her house and garden with a whole universe of ideas.

Emily opened her little book, smoothed back the page, and began to write. She wrote about flowers and love, and she wrote about the mysteries of death and the afterlife. She penned her thoughts and questions about spirituality. Emily wrote with compassion. She had no idea that one day her poems would be collected into books and

## Chapter 1

published, to be read and admired by people all over the world. In fact, she didn't want that to happen.

"This is my letter to the world," begins one of her poems. It ends, "Judge tenderly of me."[1] It was important to her to share her ideas through poetry, but she wished not to be judged harshly for her ideas.

While she asks for tenderness, she also speaks of herself as something dangerous and explosive. One poem begins:

> My Life had stood—a Loaded Gun—
> In Corners—till a Day
> The Owner passed—identified—
> And carried Me away—

and ends:

> For I have but the power to kill
> Without—the power to die.[2]

These poems reveal a hint of the contradictions in her life. She was sweet but rebellious, shy but bold, sensitive yet strong.

People have interpreted her life many different ways. Some have told her story through dramatic tales of lost love or insanity. Surviving relatives and biographers have argued over how to explain many elements of Dickinson's life. Even now, many scholars are finding new ways to understand Dickinson's existence.

The letters Dickinson received from others were burned after her death. Yet many of her letters to others survived, and she left her poems: over 1,700 pieces of her life. These poems provide further insight into the private world of the poet. The poems tell the world about the life of Emily Dickinson.

## What Is Poetry?

*Poetry* is difficult to define because the word continually takes on new meaning. It can't be defined by a particular format or style, and it means different things to many people in different cultures. Essentially, poetry is the expression of life captured through language so that the reader or listener who experiences it may, at the very least, catch a glimpse of the writer's life. It is a way for the poet to say, "Hey! Look at what I experience. See what I see through my eyes." Each poet brings his or her own unique idea to poetry.

From the beginning of civilization, humans told stories and passed these stories down from generation to generation through the oral tradition. In the days before literacy and the printing press, telling stories was the most logical way to share. Some of these early tales were worked into verse, which made the remembering easier and the telling more lyrical. In the classic Greek epic poem *The Odyssey*, Homer tells the tale of Odysseus and his long journey to return home from the Trojan War. Other epic poems also recount tales of heroic journeys and war, such as Homer's *Iliad* or *Mahabharata*, a Sanskrit epic from India. Ancient epic poems have survived through the centuries, and new ones continue to be written.

At some point, poets turned to specific forms to express ideas. These forms are represented in different types of poetry such as ballads, sonnets, and haiku. In Western literature, poets began using structure, rhyme, and rhythm to convey meaning. Lyric poetry, whose name comes from the word *lyre* (a musical instrument) because the poems were originally created to be sung, became popular during the Middle Ages. Lyric poetry can also be read, however. The poems were sometimes spoken dramatically. The speaker of the poem would address an intended audience, sharing ideas, feelings, and thoughts. Lyric poetry was often composed by a troubadour, a poet who performed for royalty and sometimes traveled from court to court. Lyric poems are still written today, and many of the major poets of the nineteenth and twentieth centuries wrote lyric poems. In the United States,

Homer traveled throughout Greece reciting his poetry.

Edgar Allan Poe, Robert Frost, and Emily Dickinson all wrote lyric poems.

Within the context of forms, poetry can follow a specific set of rules. By the thirteenth century, Italians developed a poetry form called the sonnet—from the word *sonneto*, which means "little song." An Italian sonnet is divided into two parts. The first part has eight lines and usually details a problem. Then the second part has six lines, which contain the solution. These sections of the poems—and the sections of all poems—are called stanzas.

In the sixteenth century, the English adopted the sonnet and elaborated on the form. They created three stanzas of four lines with alternating rhymes, with a final stanza of two rhyming lines. Shakespeare is well known for using this form.

Poetry took on many other forms. In Japan, haiku was developed. These small poems consisted of three lines of poetry. The first line has five syllables, the second line has seven syllables, and the third line has five syllables. Haikus are short, so this form suggests a brief image for the reader. In turn, the reader can then bring his or her own experience to the image presented.

By the twentieth century, many poets rejected traditional forms and rhyming lines. In this "free verse," no specific rhyming style or format is used. This style became very popular with the Beat Generation, a group of poets in the 1950s and 1960s who rejected traditional style and academic standards for poetry and designed an experimental style of their own. Some of these writers were Jack Kerouac, Allen Ginsberg, and Gary Snyder.

With the turn of the twenty-first century came a great deal of diversity in poets and poetry. Some poets were using very traditional forms, and some were making up their own forms—poems ranging from sonnets to rap and other popular songs were being written. Some poets were returning to the days of performance. In a poetry slam, an idea or a group of words is given; then the poets have a set amount of time to create a poem to fit the requirements. When the time is up, all the poets stand up and perform their newly improvised poem.

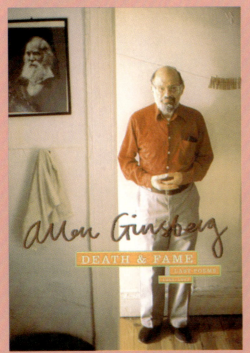

The enduring human condition as experienced in changing times has given poetry wide appreciation across cultures and throughout time.

The earliest image of Emily is in Otis A. Bullard's 1840s portrait of the three Dickinson children: Emily (left) at age nine, Austin at ten, and Lavinia at six.

# Chapter 2

## Growing Up with Life and Death

Amherst, Massachusetts, was a small but lively town in the 1830s. Most people worked as merchants or in agriculture. There was also a growing academic community. People lived in houses without modern plumbing or electricity. Instead they relied on wood and coal for heat and whale oil lamps for light. For transportation, they walked or used horses and buggies.

Emily Elizabeth Dickinson was born on December 10, 1830. She joined her older brother, William Austin (he went by his middle name), born in 1829. Her younger sister, Lavinia Norcross, or Vinnie, was born in 1833. The three children lived with their parents, Edward Dickinson and Emily Norcross Dickinson. Amherst was a growing college town that had been named after Jeffrey Amherst, a hero from the French and Indian War. The Dickinson family had lived in the area for many years; their ancestors had come to Massachusetts in 1659 and established a town called Hadley. Nathaniel and Ann Gull Dickinson had left England in the 1630s to find a place where they could freely practice their Puritan religion. Early life in Hadley included skirmishes between the settlers and the indigenous people.

By the nineteenth century, the town of Amherst had settled down. Emily was one of many descendants of Nathaniel and Ann. Emily's

# Chapter 2

grandfather, Samuel Fowler Dickinson, was an influential attorney who believed in promoting education. He married Lucretia Gunn, and they had nine children together. Their oldest son, Edward, was Emily's father. Samuel created the Amherst Academy in 1814, a private classical school. This is the school that Emily would attend. He also cofounded Amherst College, which was originally created to educate ministers and missionaries. Samuel built the family house, the Dickinson Homestead, in 1813. It is still standing today.

Though Samuel Fowler Dickinson was ambitious, he didn't always handle his money properly. He wanted to own land and make financial contributions to the schools he'd helped to establish, and he did this by taking out a large mortgage on his house. The donations put a huge financial strain on him and his family.

Emily's mother, Emily Norcross, grew up near Amherst in the town of Monson. Her father, Joel Norcross, was a successful landowner and businessman. His wife, Betsy Fay, had nine children, but not all of them lived until adulthood. Emily Norcross, the oldest daughter, helped her mother as much as she could.

In 1826, Samuel's son Edward attended a lecture on chemistry in Monson. There he met the young Emily Norcross. After the lecture, Edward and Emily exchanged letters, and Edward asked Emily to marry him. In 1828, they were married. He began establishing his law practice and became treasurer at Amherst College. Later he would be a senator for a short time. Edward was determined to be a successful businessman and handle his money more prudently than his father had. He found his father's sometimes reckless business transactions embarrassing. He was determined to reestablish the family's wealth.

The letters that survive from his lifetime reveal that Edward tended to worry excessively about the health of his family. He warned his wife to stay away from the night air, which people of this time believed to be dangerous. He also kept a close eye on his children and put them in bed when they were not feeling well. Though Edward's fears may seem rather extreme by today's standards, at that time it probably

*Growing Up with Life and Death*

Emily's grandmother, Lucretia Gunn Dickinson, was Edward Dickinson's mother.

## Chapter 2

made more sense. This was the era before vaccinations and antibiotics for diseases and infections. A mild illness could turn into pneumonia or some other deadly disease. Edward's excessive concerns about his family's health, though, revealed his need for security.

Emily's mother was quiet and hardworking, and she often felt overwhelmed by the demands of running a house. At this time before electricity and plumbing, doing basic chores took a great deal of effort. Cooking was done on an open fire or on a coal- or wood-burning stove. All the dishes and laundry had to be done by hand. She didn't complain about the amount of work she had to do, but she had little time for much else.

After the birth of Vinnie, Emily's mother became sick. Emily was sent to spend time with her Aunt Lavinia in the Norcross family home in Monson. There she experienced a great deal of warmth and devotion from her young aunt. Letters from this time reveal that Lavinia was charmed by her well-behaved and sweet little niece. Finally, Emily was experiencing the affection and attention she wanted from grown-ups. When Emily had to return home, Aunt Lavinia became sad and lonely. The friendship that began between Lavinia and Emily lasted for many years.

Growing up in a bustling New England village of Amherst provided many opportunities for Emily to interact with others. Since the Dickinsons were a prominent family in the community, they participated in some of the academic and social activities there, such as commencement ceremonies and academic lectures at Amherst College. They also attended the First Church (Congregational) regularly.

There were some challenges, however. Grandfather Samuel had purchased property without having enough money to pay all the mortgages. To pay off his debts, he had to sell the Homestead, the lovely brick house in which Edward had been raised. Emily's father felt the house should belong to the Dickinsons again. Working out a deal with other family members, Edward managed to purchase half the house for his family to live in. The other half was occupied by another family. It wasn't a perfect solution, but it was home for young Emily.

## Growing Up with Life and Death

In her early years, Emily probably attended West Center District School, but she may have spent many days at home because of Edward's fears for his young daughter. What she didn't learn at school, Emily learned from her family.

Emily's parents loved their children—though, as was common in that era, they kept a certain amount of emotional distance. Emily's mother seemed especially remote to Emily. Her father seemed overly stern at times. Parents felt that strictness was necessary in raising children to be moral and productive adults. Also, since many children died of diseases, many parents tried not to make strong attachments with their children. Part of the reason Emily felt detachment, though, may have come from Emily herself. She was a sensitive child who thrived in the connections she made with her family and friends. She felt a very strong need to be close to those around her. Many years later, Emily would tell a friend, "I never had a mother."[1] This statement reflects how Emily interpreted her mother's lack of affection as a lack of love.

Despite her parents' distance, Emily grew up with some emotional support. She helped her mother with housework and learned about gardening, a passion for both Emily and her mother. Young Emily also spent a great deal of time wandering around in the woods near her home. She was deemed sensitive and intelligent by her family. Emily was very close to Austin and Vinnie. She looked to Austin for guidance, and, as they grew, he recommended and shared books with her—including ones that didn't always meet her father's approval. As Emily grew older, she went on outings with her sister to visit friends.

As Edward began to increase his income, he wanted a larger house for his family. In 1840 they moved to West Street, where they would live until 1855. The Dickinson family had the spacious house all to themselves, and the grounds had room for a garden, an orchard, and grapevines. Austin planted a grove of pines as well.

The upstairs windows in the back looked out over Amherst's graveyard. She watched many burials from her house, including ones for people she knew. Emily was troubled by the memories of those she lost

# Chapter 2

and the images of grief and death she observed from her house. Her physical closeness to death would, in part, contribute to the theme of death found in many of her poems.

Something else haunted young Emily, her family, and the people who lived in Amherst. In the middle of the nineteenth century, in Massachusetts, 22 percent of the deaths were caused by tuberculosis. Even a simple cold with a persistent cough could be a sign of impending death. This disease had no known cure, and how it was transmitted was not fully understood. This killer lurked in many households in the community, taking its toll on young and old alike.

The Dickinson family feared it could visit their house as well.

# Tuberculosis

Tuberculosis, caused by *Mycobacterium tuberculosis*, is a debilitating infection that was once a leading cause of death worldwide. *Mycobacterium* is an airborne bacteria that usually infects a person's lungs, though other organs in the body can be damaged as well. It can spread when an actively infected person coughs or sneezes. Yet it usually takes an extended amount of time in the company of an infected person before someone catches the disease. Not everyone who is infected develops an active case of tuberculosis.

The disease has been around for a long time. The first evidence of tuberculosis was found in Egyptian mummies. The disease is also recorded in Greek literature and history. Early on, it wasn't fully understood. Since it wasn't yet known that illness is caused and spread by bacteria and viruses, many believed that diseases appeared spontaneously.

Strangely, tuberculosis, which was also called consumption, was considered a disease of status. At first it seemed that many of the victims were of the upper class and famous. Some even considered that tuberculosis made someone more artistically creative, since many talented people—including writers—fell victim to the disease. Obviously, this idea had no truth behind it. Also, tuberculosis was romanticized in women because it made them pale and thin, which represented beauty to some. This view of the disease changed as people realized that anyone could contract the disease, regardless of the fame or social status of the victim.

Tuberculosis spread through New England during the eighteenth and nineteenth centuries. The terms *consumption* or *wasting disease* were used to describe tuberculosis because, as the disease progressed, the victim's body became thin and pale. In fact, some people even believed that those suffering from tuberculosis were victims of vampires. In 1800, the disease was so widespread that 16 out of every 1,000 New Englanders died. As the century progressed and the United States expanded westward, the disease followed the population.

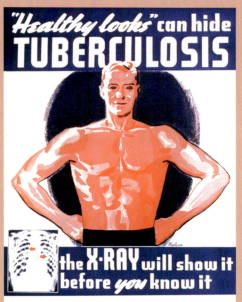

A 1930s National Tuberculosis Association poster urges people to get tested for the disease.

By the eighteenth century, an English doctor, Benjamin Marten, made a remarkable conclusion for the time. He speculated that consumption was caused by some sort of tiny organism. He also realized that spending extended time with someone sick with consumption could help the disease spread.

During the nineteenth century, when tuberculosis took the lives of thousands, important medical breakthroughs were made. A German student of botany who had the disease, Hermann Brehmer, went to the Himalaya Mountains because his doctor advised him to seek a healthier climate. He returned from the journey cured and eventually wrote a dissertation on how to cure tuberculosis. He developed the idea of sanatoriums. In these places, which were originally built in high elevations, patients could be exposed to fresh air, and they would be fed large quantities of healthy food. Sanatoriums proved to work in many cases.

Around 1865, Jean-Antoine Villemin discovered that tuberculosis could be passed between humans and animals. This link provided more proof that a specific microorganism was the culprit for the disease. Later, in 1882, German physician Robert Koch found that he could see *Mycobacterium tuberculosis* by using a staining technique. This was an important discovery because it allowed the bacteria to be isolated and studied under the microscope.

In the twentieth century, a vaccine was developed, and during World War II, a chemotherapy regime was created to kill the bacteria and halt the progress of the disease. In addition, a strong antibiotic was created. In 1944 the first human test was done with great success. A critically ill patient recovered. Antibiotics combined with the continued use of sanatoriums to isolate patients and help them fight the disease with fresh air and a healthy diet caused a decline in tuberculosis deaths. Since the 1950s, more antibiotics have been developed to fight the disease.

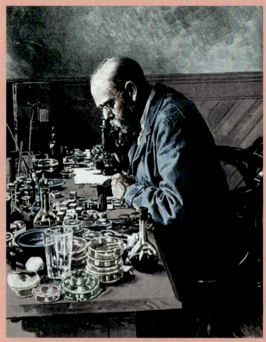

Robert Koch used a staining technique to view the tuberculosis bacteria, *Mycobacterium tuberculosis*.

In the twenty-first century, tuberculosis is no longer a major threat in developed countries. However, it is still a problem in underdeveloped countries where medical care isn't always available. Also, people with HIV, who are more prone to infection, often suffer from tuberculosis. Finally, some antibiotic-resistant strains of the disease have developed.

Many people are working to make tuberculosis a disease of the past, but over 50 million people still contract the disease every year. Though it might not be the worldwide killer it once was, tuberculosis is far from eradicated.

A page from Emily Dickinson's herbarium, which she began while attending Amherst Academy.

# Chapter 3

## Studying Nature

Following the trend to promote education for girls, Amherst Academy began accepting female students in 1838 after a fire destroyed the Amherst Female Seminary. Two years later, when she was ten, Emily began attending Amherst Academy, for Edward Dickinson believed that both of his daughters should be educated. Though girls were encouraged to learn, they were generally taught subjects that reinforced such traditional roles as mothers and teachers. Because of innovative teachers in Amherst, Emily's education was broader than most. Emily enjoyed school and was considered a good student. She learned English, Latin, botany, geology, history, and math. Natural theology (the understanding of God through nature) and biology were encouraged at the school. In addition, Emily had the opportunity to learn about science and botany because prominent scientists would give free lectures at the college. One of the textbooks that Emily used was *Elements of Mental Philosophy* by Thomas Cogswell Upham, which was a book that covered some early ideas of psychology.

It is not known exactly when Emily first began writing poetry. Some believe it might have been as early as age fourteen. It is known, however, that she was influenced by her education at Amherst Academy. A science teacher and later Amherst College president—Edward Hitchcock

## Chapter 3

Amherst College was founded by Emily's grandfather.

—lectured on geology. Emily's knowledge of science can be seen in the following poem: "The Butterfly's Assumption Gown / In Chrysoprase Apartments hung / This Afternoon put on—."[1] Chrysoprase is a green type of chalcedony, a translucent milky type of quartz. This shows that Emily had an understanding of geology and could mix it with more traditional images in a poem.

The theme of seasons began taking on symbolic value in Dickinson's poems. For example, spring sometimes symbolized birth or rebirth, and winter sometimes symbolized death. These ideas worked well with her growing love of her garden and the seasonal changes she observed with her flowers. There is evidence that Hitchcock's *Religious Lectures on Peculiar Phenomena in the Four Seasons* influenced this development.

Emily studied Latin, and her understanding of the language is apparent in her poems, where she uses Latin names for flowers and plants. In one early poem, Emily begins with a formal Latin saying: "*Sic transit Gloria mundi.*"[2] The proverb means "Thus passes the glory of the world" and is more commonly translated "Fame is fleeting."

Though Dickinson had an excellent introduction to a classical education, she continued to miss school because of health problems. Many times she had to withdraw from classes or take long absences. She continued to worry her family because she suffered from bad colds and coughs. She also became very thin.

While at Amherst Academy, Emily created an herbarium, which is a book containing specimens of plants labeled with Latin or familiar names. In a letter to a friend, Emily wrote: "Have you made a herbarium yet? I hope you will if you have not, it would be such a treasure to you. If you do, perhaps I can make some addition to it from flowers growing around here."[3] Emily collected, dried, and labeled plants she found around Amherst. She walked in the woods for hours, searching for the perfect specimen for her collection.

Botany provided a great deal of joy for Emily. The time spent outside searching in the woods also proved beneficial to both her physical and emotional health. Her thoughts about these excursions are revealed in a poem: "Who robbed the Woods / The trusting Woods," in which the speaker of the poem goes to find specimens that "He grasped—he bore away—."[4] In another poem, her knowledge of the parts of plants is revealed: "The Gentian has a parched Corolla—."[5] The gentian is a type of flower, and the corolla refers to the collective petals of the flower.

In school, Emily distinguished herself as a talented writer of essays. The Reverend Daniel T. Fiske, one of her teachers, would recall that Emily's "compositions were strikingly original; and in both thought and style seemed beyond her years, and always attracted much attention in the school and, I am afraid, excited not a little envy."[6]

Edward Hitchcock, president of Amherst College

## Chapter 3

Her brother Austin also admired Emily's writing. He noted: "Her compositions were unlike anything ever heard—and always produced a sensation—both with the scholars and Teachers—her imagination sparkled—and she gave it free rein."[7]

Emily contributed to *Forest Leaves*, a collection of handwritten stories put together by some of the students. She was remembered for her wit and imagination in the stories she created.

As Emily began to blossom, many of those close to her were dying. In 1842, Lavinia, the four-year-old daughter of Aunt Lavinia and Uncle Loring Norcross, died. In the following years, some of the mothers of Emily's friends caught tuberculosis and died. Then in April 1844, Emily's second cousin Sophia Holland died of typhus. Emily had a certain curiosity about death. She felt she would somehow gain something by being with Sophia while she was ill. Emily was allowed into the room for a short time to watch over her cousin. She later wrote: "I shed no tear, for my heart was too full to weep. But after she was laid in her coffin & I felt I could not call her back again I gave way to a fixed melancholy."[8]

After the death of Sophia, it is believed that Emily suffered both physically and mentally, though her exact symptoms are not known. She was sent to recuperate in Boston with Lavinia and Loring.

Later, in 1844, a local Amherst woman committed suicide by throwing herself into a well. Emily grew to believe that a long healthy life wasn't a guarantee and that she should enjoy the moments she had. This closeness to death is revealed in many of her poems, including "Safe in Their Alabaster Chambers," about those awaiting the afterlife in their coffins, and "Because I could not stop for Death," whose speaker meets "death," a polite being who "kindly stopped for me."[9]

After she returned from Boston in June, Emily met her first close school friend, Abiah Palmer Root. Abiah was wearing dandelions in her hair—one of Emily's favorite flowers. Abiah was working on a novel, an undertaking that greatly impressed Emily. Soon Abiah, Emily, and some other girls—Abby Wood, Harriet Merrill, and Sarah Tracy—began to spend time together and write letters to one another.

## Studying Nature

In her letters, Emily remarked, "Abby was studious, Harriet was 'making fun,' and Sarah was 'as consistent and calm and lovely as ever.'"[10] Still, these school friendships didn't last. In the years that followed, the girls finished their time at the academy and went their separate ways. Emily wanted to stay close to her friends, and their drifting apart upset her.

Around 1847, during this time of growth and change, a daguerreotype of Emily was taken. Edward Dickinson was anxious to have images of all the members of his family. He considered it important in case someone died.

A daguerreotype is an early kind of photograph that was introduced by Louis Daguerre in 1839. A person posing for a daguerreotype had to sit still for a prolonged period so that the film could develop, and one can see the resulting discomfort in the picture of adolescent Emily as she looks with a very serious face at the viewer. She is wearing a dark patterned dress and is holding a bouquet of violets in one hand. This image of Emily may be the only photographic image of the poet; if not, it is one of only two. Her naturally wavy hair is pulled back straight, and she looks thin as if after an illness. Her family wasn't completely happy with the image and found it not really representative of the Emily they knew. Still, it is a picture of what the poet looked like as a teenager.

Louis Daguerre invented an early photography technique called the daguerreotype.

Years later, when asked for a picture by an editor, Emily provided the following description of herself: "I have no portrait now, but, am

## Chapter 3

small, like a wren; and my hair is bold like a chestnut bur; and my eyes, like the sherry in the glass, that the guest leaves."[11] This shows how Emily viewed herself, and though she was accurate in many respects—her hair was auburn and her eyes were brown—she may not have been as small as she noted. She was actually about five feet four inches tall, which, for a nineteenth-century woman (generally shorter than modern women), was about average height.

About the time the daguerreotype was taken of Emily, she finished her education at Amherst Academy. Many of her friends went on to other schools, and Emily wanted to do the same. After begging her father for a chance to leave Amherst to go away to school, he finally relented. Would young Emily be able to handle being away from her beloved home?

# Footprints of the Past

Edward Hitchcock, who was first a professor and later the president of Amherst College, was born in Deerfield, Massachusetts in 1793. From a young age, he had an interest in science. In 1811, he had the opportunity to observe a comet through a telescope, and this inspired him to become an astronomer. Unfortunately, just before he was to go to Harvard, his eyes suffered, apparently from an attack of the mumps, and he felt he could no longer pursue his dream. He worked as the principal at Deerfield Academy from 1815 to 1819. There he met Orra White, a talented illustrator and artist. He left the academy and in 1821 was ordained as Congregationalist pastor. That same year he married Orra. She would accompany her husband on many of his scientific expeditions, creating sketches of his findings.

Edward Hitchcock was a scientist who studied geology and fossils. He was the president of Amherst College while Emily was a teen. He taught the value of observing and appreciating nature.

Hitchcock left the ministry to become a professor of chemistry and natural history at Amherst College. He was one of the scientists who established the study of geology in America. In 1832 he created one of the first geological maps of the states of Massachusetts and Rhode Island. He also founded what would eventually become the American Association for the Advancement of Science. Though he couldn't pursue his dream to become an astronomer, Hitchcock still observed the wonders of the sky. He wrote an account of the Great Leonoid Meteor Storm of 1833 in an article published in the *American Journal of Science*.

In 1835, after strange fossilized footprints were found on some shale flagstones in Greenfield, Massachusetts, Hitchcock was notified, and he searched local quarries in the Connecticut Valley for additional evidence. He wrote an article for the *American Journal of Science* announcing the findings of an ancient fossilized bird. Many scientists didn't believe him at first, but as he continued to do his studies and found more and more evidence, more scientists became convinced that Hitchcock was right. Well, almost right. Because the understanding of dinosaurs wasn't what it is today, Hitchcock thought he had found ancient footprints of a large, flightless bird—something like an ostrich. What he had actually found were dinosaur footprints. He collected more than 20,000 of these dinosaur fossil footprints. Now many scientists believe that dinosaurs were the ancestors of modern birds, and some may have been feathered.

In 1845, Hitchcock became the president of the college and a professor of natural theology and geology. He held the title of presidency until 1854. As president, he helped the college out of financial problems and established a solid scientific background for the college. He wrote a textbook on geology that was used for over thirty years. Hitchcock did seek to make religion and science complementary. He used biblical interpretations to help back up his scientific findings. Sometimes he found contradictions between religion and science, but he sought to keep an open mind about the natural world even if it didn't always fit into his religious beliefs. He was an innovative scientist whose curiosity led him to many fascinating discoveries.

One of his biggest interests was ichnology, the study of trace fossils such as footprints, nests, or dung—fossils that are related to the animal but are not the body parts of the animal itself. Hitchcock may have been one of the first people to use the term *ichnology* in an article written in 1858. He also discovered the dinosaur *Anomoepus intermedius*, from the Triassic period. This dinosaur is identified only by its fossilized tail prints, which Hitchcock documented. At the time, Hitchcock had no idea he had discovered a species of dinosaur. He published his fossil findings in a two-volume collection, *Ichnology of New England*.

Hitchcock also made other interesting scientific discoveries. He did research on anthropometry, the study of measuring the human body. His research became the basis for studies in physical education.

Hitchcock's work continues today. The Pratt Museum of the Amherst College Museum of Natural History houses the largest dinosaur footprint collection in the world. The Hitchcock Ichnology Collection is used by scientists around the world who want to study the past.

Hitchcock died in 1864, leaving behind a legacy of discovery.

Hitchcock discovered the *Anomoepus intermedius* dinosaur through a fossilized tail print.

A sketch of Emily Dickinson by an unknown artist.

# Chapter 4

## Away from Home and Back Again

In 1847, Emily moved away from home to attend Mount Holyoke Female Seminary, a four-story brick building nine miles outside of Amherst. There were 235 students that year and 12 teachers. Her education consisted of a highly regimented day filled with academic classes and domestic duties. According to a history of the school, "the school day lasted more than 16 hours. Between 5 A.M.—the required wake-up time—and bedtime at 9:15 P.M., the Seminary was run on a strict schedule."[1]

At Mount Holyoke, Emily continued to study a variety of subjects. The school was run by Mary Lyon, an innovator of female education. Like the education Emily received at Amherst Academy, her studies included science and other subjects that were not traditionally taught to young women. Emily was fortunate to go to a school where her intelligence was fostered.

Mary Lyon felt that science was an important topic for young women to learn. She had students conduct scientific experiments in a laboratory so that they would have practical, hands-on experience. Among the sciences taught at the school were geology, chemistry, and astronomy. Emily studied hard, for she wanted to do well. She found schoolwork interesting, but she also wanted to keep her family happy

# Chapter 4

and not disgrace her father with poor grades.

The schedule at Mount Holyoke included classes in which students memorized materials, analyzed books, and wrote compositions. Students also exercised every day with a required walk (even in winter) and calisthenics. They also formed domestic work circles to complete housework required at the seminary. One of Emily's domestic duties was to put the knives on the tables and then wash them after meals. This work didn't seem too demanding for her—she was accustomed to helping out her mother at home.

Mary Lyon ran the Mount Holyoke Female Seminary. She believed in teaching young women a variety of topics including geology, chemistry, and astronomy.

At first, Emily missed her house and her family. In a letter to Abiah, she wrote about being homesick: "You may laugh at the idea that I cannot be happy when away from home, but you must remember that I have a very dear home and that this is my first trial in the way of absence for any length of time in my life."[2]

While away at school, Emily was put under a great deal of pressure to "convert." Religious devotional activities were part of the daily life at school. In this highly Christian community, it was believed that in order for a person to be saved as a Christian, the person had to express his or her beliefs in front of others. At Mount Holyoke, activities were designed to help pupils convert to Christianity. The school planned a prayer and fast for Christmas Eve. Unlike the celebratory Christmas of contemporary times, Christmas then was a time of contemplation. Mary Lyon met with all those who hadn't converted; this group of students was referred to as "the impenitent." Specifically, she prayed with the group in hopes that they would convert. Though Emily attended church with her family growing up, she hadn't had a conversion experience.

There are legends about what happened to Emily during this time. Her niece, Martha Dickinson Bianchi, said that Emily alone held out and wasn't converted. Yet there is strong evidence that others didn't convert as well. The pressure to convert lasted throughout the school year. Emily was even given a roommate who was to try to save her. In her surviving letters, Emily had noted that she should accept Christ, but something in her would not allow this to happen. She felt she had to have a genuine sense of something spiritual to join the saved. Despite the immense pressure that was put upon her, Emily resisted and refused to be converted—even after her entire family had done so.

Emily left Mount Holyoke Female Seminary before the end of her first school year. Her father decided she should leave because he was worried about her health. Emily had caught another bad cold and had a persistent cough. These were potentially deadly symptoms, so extra caution was taken. Even with her homesickness earlier in the year, Emily had grown to love school and was sorry to leave early.

Emily settled down at home to help her mother with the housework. Since her mother was often sick, Emily found that taking on the extra house chores was a burden. It was her first experience with the drudgery of women's work. Bread making, however, became one of Emily's specialties. In a letter to Abiah in 1850, Emily writes of her pride in baking bread and reveals her sense of humor: "Twin loaves of bread have just been born into the world under my auspices,— fine children, image of their mother; and here my dear friend, is the *glory*."[3] Yet Emily's life wasn't strictly full of chores. She also played the piano. She liked to stay up late and improvise, creating original songs for herself and her family.

Emily also continued to read and study and consider ideas about literature and religion. During this time, a young man who was studying law and staying at the Dickinson house had a profound influence on Emily and her desire to be a poet. Benjamin Franklin Newton acted

## Chapter 4

as a tutor for her and gave her a copy of Ralph Waldo Emerson's poetry. Emerson's work deeply moved Emily. She found certain elements in his poetry that she would use in her own. Emerson focused on the natural world, and he sought to be original in his thoughts and ideas. A part of the transcendentalist movement in American literature, he strove to reject old ideas about spirituality. Because she considered her independence important, Emily didn't identify with the transcendentalist movement; however, her poems reveal its influence, specifically her poems about nature and spirituality.

In addition to introducing her to the works of Emerson, Newton encouraged her to pursue her own passion for poetry. Many years later, when Emily wrote to an editor, she said, "My dying tutor told me that he would like to live till I had been a poet."[4] That tutor was Newton. Unfortunately, he didn't reach his goal. He died in 1853 of tuberculosis. He was only thirty-two.

Another friend, Henry Vaughan Emmons, also influenced her writing. He and Dickinson critiqued each other's work when Emmons was the editor for a literary magazine in Amherst College. Emmons wrote inspiring essays on writing and poetry. His essay "Poetry, the Voice of Sorrow" appealed to Emily's sense of destiny—the essay argued that certain people have a gift for poetry and should pursue their talents. Emily took this to heart.

Housekeeping, music, and literature were not the only things that occupied young Emily's life. The pressure to save her soul by accepting Christ continued for Emily, and she continued to stand out among her family and friends by resisting. In a letter to her friend Jane Humphrey, she wrote: "Christ is calling everyone here, all my companions have answered, even my darling Vinnie believes she loves, and trusts him, and I am standing alone in rebellion."[5]

After Austin graduated from Amherst College, he went to Boston to teach. Emily missed her big brother. She spent time writing letters, writing poems, and reading. With recommendations from Austin, Emily read new literature. At that time, British literature was popular in America, so Emily took the opportunity to read the great works coming from across the Atlantic. Sometimes Emily's father didn't approve of what his children read, but Emily continued to read what she liked. She found her books comforting.

Emily read the works of Robert Browning and Elizabeth Barrett Browning, popular poets of the time. Elizabeth Barrett Browning had a special significance for Emily because she was a critically acclaimed poet who had overcome obstacles—poor health and a prevailing belief that women couldn't write as well as men. The novel *Jane Eyre* by Charlotte Brontë was also an inspiration. In the novel, a young woman, Jane Eyre, works as a governess for a mysterious man, Rochester. After Rochester and Jane Eyre fall in love, Jane finds out a terrible secret about Rochester's past. She flees with nowhere to go and is befriended by three respectable siblings. The two sisters, Diana and Mary Rivers, become her friends, and their brother, St. John, asks Jane to marry him and join him with his missionary work. Jane again must make a choice. Though the novel has many similarities to romantic novels of the period, Jane Eyre is a brave and independent female character. The novel was originally published under the pseudonym Currer Bell, and many speculated on whether the author was male or female. Emily loved the novel and even named the large dog her father bought her Carlo—after St. John's dog in the novel.

Later, after she heard of the death of Charlotte Brontë, Emily wrote a poem about her. It begins with a description of Brontë's headstone: "All overgrown by cunning moss / All interspersed with weed, / The little cage of 'Currer Bell' / In quiet Haworth laid."[6] This poem, along with others that Emily would write, shows how important it was for Emily to express her feelings for those who had an impact in her life. She never met any of the Brontë sisters (a talented trio of writers), but their work meant much to her.

Emily also read Henry Wadsworth Longfellow's *Kavanagh*, a popular novel about life in New England. One of the books that had a more profound influence on Emily was X. B. Saintine's *Picciola*. The novel

# Chapter 4

tells of an imprisoned man who finds a small plant growing between the stones of the fortress where he is held. By taking care of the plant, the character finds spiritual redemption. The novel reminded Emily of her own fortress she was developing within the walls of her house and her garden, the place where her imagination soared. The plant nurtured in the novel was not unlike the plants and the poems that Emily nurtured.

Emily did have health problems. Most specifically she continued to have a persistent cough and weight loss, two common symptoms of tuberculosis. Is it possible that she had this disease? Many scholars believe that she did indeed have tuberculosis. In 1851, she went to Boston to see a doctor who prescribed glycerin, a remedy for her cough. She also worked to put on weight so that her family would worry less. Eventually, she was able to send the disease into remission, yet the fear of death must have sat very close to her and her family. Many people she knew had been killed by this disease. Would Emily be next?

## American Transcendentalism

Transcendentalism was a spiritual, literary, and philosophical movement in nineteenth-century America, primarily in New England. In an effort to separate themselves from the past and from European ideas, a group of American writers and thinkers sought to create an "original" American belief system.

To transcend something means to move past or go beyond it. Transcendentalists wanted to move beyond old ideas. The reaction came about in an effort to disconnect with the traditional and strict teachings of the Unitarian Church that had neglected human spiritual need. They sought new ideas about spirituality and life. Since transcendentalism wasn't a religion, there were different points of view on the essential elements of the movement. However, transcendentalism is universally viewed as a type of idealism.

Transcendentalism strove to disconnect from the adherence to sensory world. In other words, the transcendentalists felt people put too much emphasis on what was obvious, such as what someone sees or hears. Instead, transcendentalists valued intuition above all things. They believed that humans are basically good, but we achieve greatness through our independent thoughts and actions. Therefore, what we do is an important part of who we are.

Transcendentalists also seek a connection with the natural world based on an experience. The natural world provided a means to experience something symbolic or even spiritual. Many transcendentalist writers went into a natural setting to experience something profound that they would receive directly (rather than what they would learn from someone else). They sought to make a connection between the natural world of the earth around them and the supernatural world of spirituality.

Many people involved in the transcendentalist movement also became involved in the women's rights and abolitionist movements. They felt that all people, regardless of gender or race, had a right to the same freedoms that others enjoyed. It was an essential part of being human. Some also believed that

Ralph Waldo Emerson is considered the founder of the transcendentalist movement. He wrote essays on many topics, including the observation of nature and the power of the natural world.

it was okay to break the law if necessary to back up their beliefs. For example, many transcendentalist abolitionists were involved in the Underground Railroad—a system for smuggling African-American slaves out of slave states. Others organized legal protests and demonstrations.

Many writers were transcendentalists—most significantly Ralph Waldo Emerson, who wrote about the philosophy in his essays and gave a lecture on transcendentalism. In his essay "Nature," he reveals the basic ideas of transcendentalism by describing what happens when he is in the woods: "Standing on the bare ground—my head bathed by the blithe air and uplifted into infinite space—all egotism vanishes. I become a transparent eyeball; I am nothing; I see all; the currents of the Universal Being circulate through me; I am part and parcel of God."[7]

Also involved in the movement was Henry David Thoreau, whose experiences living near Walden Pond are chronicled in his work *Walden*. Walt Whitman expressed his openness and love of nature in his poetry collection *Leaves of Grass*. Other writers and thinkers who became transcendentalists include Dickinson's friend and editor Thomas Wentworth Higginson. The writings of Edgar Allan Poe, Nathaniel Hawthorne, and Emily Dickinson were all influenced on some level by American transcendentalism as well.

Transcendentalism was shunned by many mainstream religious groups; its connection to Eastern religions led some to believe that transcendentalism could be a threat to Christianity and Christian behavior. Also, the movement away from rationalism seemed reckless and based on an emotional reaction rather than on sound logic. Some of the people who expressed transcendentalism in their writing found their work shunned from publication; others had their work censored before it was published.

Later, in the twentieth century, other movements were influenced by transcendentalism. For example, the civil disobedience and advocacy for equal rights championed by the Reverend Martin Luther King Jr. and other activists in the 1950s and 1960s have their roots in nineteenth-century transcendentalism. The antiestablishment or "hippie" generation of the 1960s also has its roots in transcendentalism. This group sought to move away from the ideas of materialism and toward intuitive experiences, civil disobedience, and the free expression of self.

William Austin Dickinson, Emily's beloved older brother, was very close to his sister.

Susan Gilbert Dickinson married Austin, and they lived next door to the Homestead. She was a friend of Emily's and, over the years, read many of Emily's poems.

# Chapter 5

## Emily, the Poet

In Emily's time, every year during February, the town of Amherst celebrated Valentine's Day with festivities that included the exchange of valentine messages among young people. As they are today, valentines were sent for different reasons. Pretty heart-shaped cards with loving sentiments were popular, but other kinds of valentines were created as well—ones that made fun of the person receiving the message. Since Dickinson was both a creative and witty writer, in February 1850, she decided to write a humorous composition of a fictional meeting between a woman and a man. In the composition, Dickinson makes fun of the woman's behavior by making her far bolder than the typical women of her time. Dickinson's valentine was actually published in the Amherst College publication *The Indicator*. In 1852, she used her wit to create a Valentine poem that was sent to Elbridge Bowdoin, her father's law partner, who was thirty and unmarried. The poem, "Awake Ye Muses" calls upon Bowdoin to find a woman he can love. The poem begins solemnly, but it is clear that the writer is teasing: "Awake ye muses nine, sing me a strain divine, / unwind the solemn twine, and tie my Valentine!"[1] Dickinson wrote this poem for fun; she didn't have a crush on Bowdoin. She only wished to tease him.

## Chapter 5

These early compositions show how the young Emily—in her early twenties—was playful, social, and funny. This is very different from the reclusive woman she would one day become. Even though it was possible that she had been writing poetry since adolescence, the Bowdoin valentine was the first known example of a poem by Dickinson.

In the early 1850s, Edward Dickinson worked on bringing a railroad to Amherst. During this time, before cars, the railroad transformed transportation. It provided faster travel than using horse and buggy. Those in favor of progress, such as Edward, enthusiastically rallied for the coming of the iron horse (as it was called). In 1853 there was a celebration when the Amherst-Belchertown Railroad line became operational. Emily watched people's reactions, including her father's pride at bringing the railroad. In a letter to Austin, she wrote, "The grand railroad decision is made, and there is great rejoicing throughout this town. Everybody is wide awake, every thing is stirring, the streets are full of people walking cheeringly, and you should really be here to partake of the jubilee."[2] When the actual celebration took place, however, Emily watched from a distance—away from the crowd.

Over time, Dickinson saw the railroad and the trains an interesting way. She wrote a poem in which she makes a train seem alive:

> I like to see it lap the miles—
> And lick the Valleys up—
> And stop to feed itself at tanks—
> And then—prodigious step
>
> Around a Pile of Mountains—
> And supercilious, peer
> In shanties by the sides of roads—
> And then a quarry pare
>
> To fit its sides—[3]

## Emily, the Poet

In her twenties, Emily developed a busy social life. She attended parties and events with Vinnie. She also developed a new friendship with two sisters—Martha and Susan Gilbert. While Martha was away helping another sister, Mary, after a birth, Emily became good friends with Susan. Despite Martha's efforts, Mary died. Susan grieved the death of one sister and the absence of her other. Emily and Susan shared their troubles with each other. Their friendship was a very powerful bond for Dickinson. During this time, someone else became interested in Susan—Emily's brother, Austin.

The friendship between Austin and Susan blossomed into a romance, and soon they were in love. Their affection for each other wasn't obvious to those around them, however. They kept their courtship secret until May 1853, when they announced their engagement to Edward Dickinson. Edward was pleased; he liked Susan very much. Emily also continued to nurture her friendship with Susan, whom she admired.

Also that year, Edward Dickinson, who was involved in politics, was elected to the United States Congress. He was a member of the Whig party, a political party that was created to oppose the Democratic party; it was similar in some respects to the present-day Republican party. Vinnie and Emily's mother traveled with Edward to Washington, while Emily stayed behind. Since Austin was in Boston teaching school, Susan stayed with Emily, as did a cousin of hers—John Long Graves—whose job was to make sure the young women were safe.

In 1855, Emily made one of her rare trips outside of Amherst to Washington, D.C., with her sister and her father. They stayed at Willard's Hotel. While Vinnie enjoyed socializing, Emily found the big-city life and the more formal environment intimidating; she missed her home. She visited the U.S. Patent Office and the tomb of George Washington, which impressed her deeply.

The more interesting part of her trip came after three weeks, when Vinnie and Emily went to Philadelphia to visit relatives. In Philadelphia, Dickinson fell under the spell of the Reverend Charles

## Chapter 5

Wadsworth. She most probably heard him give a sermon in the Arch Street Presbyterian Church, where he was a popular preacher. He had great oratory skills as a preacher and was introspective and brooding in his personal life.

Before he became a minister, he wrote poetry. He continued to use his writing skills by creating strong and powerful sermons filled with imagery. This was probably one of the reasons Emily admired him. He was also a very reserved man who didn't socialize much. He had strong Calvinist views that were different than other spiritual approaches Emily knew. As she developed her own ideas about spirituality, Wadsworth was an inspiration for her.

From a meeting, a friendship developed, and some speculate that Emily was in love with Wadsworth. He was older than she and married. They met a few times in their lives and sent letters to each other, but little else is known. The letters that were sent to Emily were destroyed, and those she sent to Wadsworth have not been found.

Also in 1855, Edward Dickinson was able to buy back the Homestead—the entire house this time. He then began a huge remodeling project to enlarge it. He added a square cupola on the roof, and a conservatory (a greenhouse) that would become a very special place for Emily. The Dickinsons moved back into their family home, where Emily would stay for the rest of her life.

Austin and Sue got married in 1856. At first, Austin wanted to move west, but Edward offered him a partnership in his law firm and a piece of land to build a house next to the Homestead. The couple built a spectacular house in the Italianate style and called it the Evergreens. Sue was excited with her new life and wanted to make her marriage the best she possibly could. She was very social and wanted important friends. Over the years, she would host many parties and events at the Evergreens. These parties included famous guests, including writers and politicians.

Because her brother and good friend lived so close, Emily was able to keep her connections with those important to her without traveling far. As she grew older and less inclined to leave her house, having her family nearby became more and more important.

Emily's admiration for her sister-in-law was very powerful. She valued Sue's opinions about her writing and wanted to be her closest friend. Over the years, she sent many letters to Sue. She also wrote many poems to her sister-in-law—approximately 250—more than what she sent to anyone else. In return, Sue provided some encouragement for Emily and feedback on her poems, but at times she was also distant. She had a busy life, suffered from health problems, and faced challenges and tragedies in her family. Sue was very strong-willed and liked to be the center of attention. She may have found her sister-in-law challenging because Emily possessed a strong sense of self. All these factors contributed to a sometimes shaky relationship between the two women.

When her mother became ill again, Emily needed to spend more time taking care of domestic matters. In addition, it seems clear that Emily herself experienced some sort of crisis. She was ill, but she also seems to have suffered an emotional problem. Not much is known, but it occurred probably in 1858. A draft of a letter to someone she addresses as "Master" states: "I am ill—but grieving more that you are ill."[4] Also, in a letter she sent to her uncle, Joseph Sweetser, she states: "Much has occurred . . . so much that I stagger as I write, in its sharp remembrance."[5]

What could have caused Dickinson so much distress? This point in Dickinson's life remains a mystery, yet many people have speculated on what actually happened. The possibility of lost love, a nervous breakdown, depression, and even a combination of these are generally accepted as reasons for Emily's problems. Without real evidence, we may never know for sure.

In 1858, without telling anyone, Dickinson began making little books of her poems. These books still survive. Biographer Alfred Habegger describes her method: "Entering several poems on each sheet, which came folded from the factory, she filled four sheets and

## Chapter 5

bound them into a little booklet with needle and thread, stabbing near the fold."[6] This practice she would continue all her life, though in the final years she wasn't quite as diligent. She would write poems first in letters to friends, on scraps of paper, or on the backs of envelopes. Then she would carefully copy the poems into her books.

Outside, beyond the Homestead, progress had come to Amherst. The Evergreens had been built and the stage was set for the future. Behind all the progress and change, Emily quietly went to work writing and copying her poems. Her witty valentine poem was only the beginning; now she was writing secretly for herself.

# The Railroad

When the railroad reached Amherst in 1853, riding on rails may have seemed very modern, but it was not a new idea. The first railways were cut stone tracks that guided horse-drawn wagons in Greece and parts of the Roman Empire two thousand years before. Railroads were used again in the sixteenth century to guide wagons. Sometimes planks worked as rails to guide heavy wagons of coal. These early railroads used the energy of humans or animals to pull the load. Some used downhill tracks so that gravity could pull the load along. A braking system was used to keep the wagons from going too fast.

The railroad changed dramatically in the nineteenth century with the development of the commercial steam engine in Great Britain. Englishman George Stephenson began manufacturing steam locomotives in 1823, and iron railroads were built across Europe.

The United States was also developing railroads of its own. In 1828, the construction of the Baltimore and Ohio railway began. The B & O railroad was designed to find a faster way for goods from the Midwest to reach the East Coast. In 1830, one of the first American locomotives was built. The engine, called "Best Friend," was awkward, with a large vertical boiler. Like many early steam engines, this one had to be carefully watched to keep the steam pressure from building up and causing an explosion. In 1831, "Best Friend" exploded.

Some criticized the early railroads. Since the steam engine produced sparks and accidents occurred, some believed that train travel was dangerous and could cause fires. The rapid advancement of better and more stable steam engines and stronger rails for travel made trains safer.

By the 1830s, many railroads had been built connecting cities in New England and the Midwest. Most of these railways were funded by private investors. Meanwhile, the expansion of the United States to western territories encouraged builders to connect the continent by a railroad. In 1845, Asa Whitney, a merchant, made a trip through the West to determine a good route for a railroad. He then made a number of proposals to the U.S.

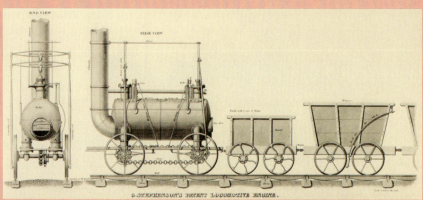
George Stephenson's steam locomotive and railroad cars were used in Europe.

government. Despite his enthusiasm, he was ignored for many years. Later, Theodore Judah would help make the railroad a reality. As an engineer, Judah was particularly interested in surveying a railroad route across the Sierra Nevada. He began appealing to the U.S. government in the 1850s for funding a transcontinental railroad. In 1862, Congress passed the Pacific Railway Act, which provided land grants for the Union Pacific Railroad and Central Pacific Railroad, and the railroad that would link Omaha, Nebraska, to Sacramento, California, was under way.

In the West, workers on the Central Pacific Railroad faced difficulty in the Sierra Nevada region. Working in winter snowstorms and blasting tunnels through the mountains made the work slow and dangerous. In the Midwest, workers on the Union Pacific Railroad faced challenges as well. Many Native Americans there felt that building the railroad violated the treaties they had made with the U.S. government. Finally, however, in 1869, the railroads met at Promontory Point, Utah.

Meanwhile, trains were made more comfortable for passengers. In the United States, George Pullman developed the first luxury sleeping car for long-distance travel. He also designed dining cars that served delicious meals (previously, most people brought their own food while traveling). In addition, hotels were built near main stations. For those who could afford it, train travel had become a comfortable experience.

By the end of the nineteenth century, electric railways, or trolleys, became popular for travel within cities. Then in the 1890s, German engineer Rudolph Diesel invented the diesel locomotive. These replaced the steam locomotive and became widely used.

Rail travel continued in the twentieth century with sleeker and faster trains. One of the most popular lines was the Super Chief, which traveled between Los Angeles and Chicago. With the invention and widespread use of the automobile and the development of passenger airlines, passenger train travel in the United States began to decline.

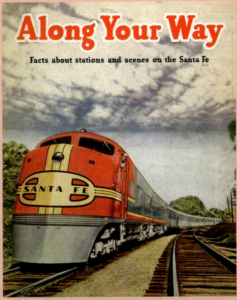

The Santa Fe Super Chief was a popular train during the middle of the twentieth century.

Though U.S. passenger trains still exist, particularly for commuting into and around cities, most trains are used for transporting freight. Passenger trains are more popular in other parts of the world, including Europe and Japan, where high-speed "bullet" trains, which go well over 150 miles per hour, are used between major cities.

Bullet train in Tokyo, Japan

A silhouette of the Dickinson family, created by a friend of Emily's at Mount Holyoke Seminary. From left to right: Emily's mother, Lavinia, Austin, Emily, and Emily's father.

# Chapter 6

## The Literary Life

In the 1850s, Dickinson became friends with Dr. Josiah G. Holland and his wife, Elizabeth Holland. Josiah Holland was an essayist and an editor of the *Springfield Daily Republican*, a newspaper that covered the news of Springfield and many surrounding areas in Massachusetts. It included poetry. The Hollands' spiritual views were more liberal than what Dickinson had grown up with. Dickinson found their views interesting. One of her greatest challenges was to remain true to her own beliefs, which she found difficult with the pressures of the church. She also felt a special connection to Elizabeth Holland because she admired the way Elizabeth interacted with her husband, and Elizabeth appreciated Dickinson's unusual and gifted writing.

Through Austin and Sue, Emily made another friendship that would last a long time—with Samuel and Mary Bowles. Samuel Bowles was also an editor of the *Springfield Daily Republican*. He was a crusader for social reform movements and friends with famous writers like Charles Dickens and Ralph Waldo Emerson. Samuel Bowles was also very handsome. Dickinson adored him, and there is some speculation that she was in love with him, and that he was the one who stole her heart. Samuel Bowles was outspoken, and, in particular, advocated rights for women and encouraged women writers. The issue of women's rights

## Chapter 6

wasn't something that Bowles and Dickinson always agreed upon. Dickinson considered herself more traditional in her views.

Both Bowles and Dickinson did share many interests, however. They both liked gardening and loved exotic plants and more familiar wildflowers. They also liked similar authors, but Bowles didn't entirely appreciate Dickinson's poetry. Though she sent him many of her poems to be published in the *Springfield Daily Republican*, he printed very few of them. For those he did publish, he first edited the format.

Dickinson and Bowles admired the work *Aurora Leigh* by British poet Elizabeth Barrett Browning. The poem examines the challenges women face in the strict gender roles of the mid-nineteenth century. It also served to empower Dickinson as a writer herself. In her copy of the poem, marks were made next to a passage about women's traditional work: "We sew, sew, prick our fingers, dull our sight."[1] The narrator goes on to discuss the kinds of things women make—slippers and stools. The passage shows the frustrations of many nineteenth-century women who were expected to do traditional women's work, which often proved to be of little value or fulfillment. Though Emily enjoyed some of her domestic duties such as baking and gardening, she also felt her chores tiresome; her poetry was her escape and her opportunity to do meaningful work.

Elizabeth Barrett Browning also had a life that Dickinson probably admired. Barrett Browning lived in Florence, Italy, with her husband and poet Robert Browning. She was interested in social issues; she was an abolitionist and an advocate for women's rights. Though she was well known for her love poems to Robert Browning, *Sonnets from the Portuguese*, her other poems—like *Aurora Leigh*—addressed issues of social change. She also wrote about slavery in America and the often appalling conditions in which poor children in London lived.

Many women were making their voices heard, including the Brontë sisters, Elizabeth Barrett Browning, and Marian Evans (who wrote under the name George Eliot). In the United States, works like Harriett Beecher Stowe's novel *Uncle Tom's Cabin* had an enormous impact on the attitudes toward slaves before the Civil War. Though Dickinson wasn't publishing her poetry, she must have gained strength from the growing popularity of female writers.

In 1860, Aunt Lavinia died from tuberculosis. Dickinson grieved over the death of her kind aunt, who had been so good to her as a child, but she also developed a stronger friendship with her aunt's daughters, Louisa and Frances, who were now adolescents. This bond continued to strengthen when her young cousins lost their father in 1863.

By 1860, the United States was divided and the threat of war was at hand. Edward Dickinson supported the war for the emancipation of the slaves. The Civil War began in 1861. Many people volunteered for the war effort or made public denouncements against slavery. In the world outside the Homestead, the United States faced the biggest challenge yet. The slaveholders of the Southern states and the free people of the Northern states disagreed on the slave issue. The Civil War was brought about by the differences in values and economic needs between these two groups. Though many people in the North were caught up in the politics of the nation, and even many women were involved in the abolitionist movement, Dickinson remained in her own world of her home and garden.

Dickinson may not have been an activist, yet the war affected her. The great suffering of many people related to the great suffering she knew personally from the loss of family and friends. Also, some of her poems were published in papers in 1864. The publication was created to raise money for the war. Though not much is known about the circumstances surrounding the publication of these poems, it is believed that it perhaps was Dickinson's small contribution to the war effort.

At some point around 1861 or 1862, Dickinson mentions in her letters to her friends that she is having some sort of emotional problem, but what the problem was remains a mystery. At that time, Charles Wadsworth moved to San Francisco to become a minister at the Calvary Presbyterian Church. His journey seemed to be as far as across the world for Dickinson. Samuel Bowles traveled to Europe for his health. Could it be possible that Emily felt abandoned by these two men who had been so important in her life? Some speculate that this was what

## Chapter 6

caused her to suffer, but we cannot be sure. There were other factors affecting her as well. Those around her were busy with their own lives and may not have been able to help Dickinson work through her problems. Austin and Sue were preoccupied with the birth of their first son, Edward, or Ned, as he was called. The boy was born June 19, 1861.

The crisis Dickinson endured caused her to turn to her poetry. She wrote like she never had before. As a result, by 1862, she had written 366 poems. She was able to take her distress and turn it into creative expression. Her poems began to become masterful in form and feeling. The poetic forms that she used were inspired by the King James Version of the Bible, and by the works of English hymn writer Isaac Watts.

Dickinson also changed around traditional rhymes and created off-rhymes—unexpected lines that draw the reader into the poem. Similarly, she used unexpected words to highlight the theme of the poem. Sometimes she would do this by putting a simple word in a complex context, or a complex word in a simple context.

Other studies done on the crises in Dickinson's life point to the characteristic mood swings associated with bipolar personality disorders. Her periods of depression are contrasted with periods of mania, or intense activity. People with bipolar disorder experience extreme depression contrasted with extreme euphoria and high energy. The possibility that Dickinson had bipolar disorder exists. Often the disorder runs in families, and Dickinson's grandfather, Samuel, was also prone to extreme mood swings. Without actual evidence, however, the diagnosis is speculation.

In 1862, one of the rare publications of Dickinson's poems occurred when Sue sent the poem "Safe in the Alabaster Chambers" to the *Springfield Daily Republican*. Sue sent a version of the poem that she preferred—Dickinson's original version, which had two stanzas. The first speaks of those in their coffins—"Safe in their Alabaster Chambers"—and the second includes images of a lively summer scene. After Emily wrote that version, Sue told her that she didn't like it. Emily then created a new second stanza that was much more profound, evoking

images of long periods of time passing—kingdoms rising and falling—
and winter above the graves:

> Grand go the Years,
> In the Crescent above them—
> Worlds scoop their Arcs—
> And Firmaments—row—
> Diadems—drop—
> Soundless as Dots,
> On a Disc of Snow.[2]

Emily preferred her second version, and this was the one she would later send to Thomas Wentworth Higginson. She had a good critical eye for her own work. Though she greatly admired her sister-in-law and listened to her advice, Emily knew that the second version of the poem was superior and ignored Sue's judgment.

In April 1862, the activist and writer Higginson wrote an article called "Letter to a Young Contributor," in which he outlined and discussed the merits of writing and seeking publication. Most significantly, in the article, he offered to read contributions by readers: "[E]very editor is always hungering and thirsting after novelties. To take the lead in bringing forward a new genius is as fascinating a privilege as that of the physician who boasted to Sir Henry Halford of having been the first man to discover the Asiatic cholera and to communicate it to the public."[3]

This article prompted Emily to send four poems and a letter to Higginson:

> Are you too deeply occupied, to say if my verse is alive?
> The Mind is so near itself—it cannot see, distinctly—and I have none to ask—
> Should you think it breathed—and had you the leisure to tell me, I should feel quick gratitude—[4]

# Chapter 6

When Higginson responded, he asked Dickinson about herself. She revealed how her solitary ways were already established: "You ask of my companions. Hills, air, and the sundown, and a dog large as myself that my father bought me. They are better than beings because they know, but do not tell."[5]

An important friendship blossomed between the poet and the writer that would last throughout Dickinson's life. Higginson's letters were among those destroyed, but we can surmise what he wrote by her answers. In a letter to him saying how much she appreciated his comments, she wrote, "I have had few pleasures so deep as your opinion, and if I tried to thank you, my tears would block my tongue."[6] Dickinson was grateful, yet Higginson's comments were not always favorable. He encouraged her to write, but discouraged her from seeking publication for most of her poems. He didn't always understand the strangeness and intensity of her work. It certainly wasn't conventional poetry for that era. He suggested changes that would make her poetry more like other poems, and he set about making little changes himself.

Dickinson looked up to Higginson for inspiration and guidance, yet her poetry was far beyond the abilities and understanding of her mentor. She largely ignored his suggestions and continued to create her unique poetry.

Higginson's reaction to Dickinson's work is revealed in an article he wrote after her death: "The impression of a wholly new and original poetic genius was as distinct on my mind at the first reading of these four poems as it is now, after thirty years of further knowledge."[7]

Dickinson had access to people who probably would have been very willing to publish her work, so many people have speculated on why she didn't. Many criticize Higginson for discouraging her. However, her reluctance to seek a publisher may have come from her own desire. Her poetry was private, and she shared it on her own terms. Friends and family would see her work when she sent a poem with a letter.

Dickinson, however, was beginning to establish herself as a poet. She was writing, and she had made friends with influential editors. Would this poet find fame?

# Emily's Mentor

Thomas Wentworth Higginson, who was born in 1823, was educated at Harvard, worked as a schoolmaster, then became a pastor. Eventually he left the church to devote his energies to freeing the slaves in America.

In order to make a difference, Higginson turned to politics and writing. In 1850, he ran for Congress as a member of the Free Soil Party. This political organization lasted only about four years, but it had important objectives: to keep slavery out of the new territories of the United States and to oppose slavery where it existed. Higginson was defeated, but his work as an abolitionist continued.

In 1854, he attempted to free Anthony Burns, a runaway slave. Discovered in Boston (part of the free North), Burns was to be sent back to his owner in the South. Higginson and other abolitionists raided the federal courthouse where Burns was kept under arrest. Higginson, with the aid of others, used a beam as a battering ram to knock down the courthouse door. The rescue was not successful. In the end, the federal government said that Burns would have to be returned to the South. Higginson was indicted for his actions, along with abolitionists Wendell Phillips and Theodore Parker.

Higginson was also involved with helping to make Kansas a free state after the controversial Kansas-Nebraska Act was passed. This act of Congress set up provisional governments in the territories of Kansas and Nebraska, and it allowed these territories to decide for themselves whether slavery should be legal there or not. This led to a great deal of outrage from the abolitionists and the Southern slave states, and was one of the key factors leading up the Civil War. The abolitionists rallied to keep Kansas free—even using violence. Higginson was one of the secret six—six men who provided funds for John Brown, an abolitionist who believed that violence was necessary to help the movement against slavery. Brown did use violence and felt it was his duty to kill those who upheld slavery. His most notorious move came in 1859. He led a small band of men and

Thomas Wentworth Higginson, an influential writer, abolitionist, women's rights activist and editor, encouraged Dickinson with her writing. The young girl on the tricycle is his daughter.

attacked a federal arsenal at Harpers Ferry, Virginia. He wanted to seize the weapons to arm slaves. Men on both sides of the attack were killed, and Brown was eventually arrested and tried for his crimes. Higginson also knew other prominent abolitionists and those involved in the Underground Railroad, including Harriet Tubman.

Higginson was also known as a proponent of women's rights. He backed the suffragettes in their struggle to achieve their right to vote. He also performed the marriage ceremony for Lucy Stone and Henry Blackwell. Since they didn't believe a woman should be under control of a man, they created their own ceremony: one that allowed husband and wife equal rights and the wife's option to keep her birth name.

During the Civil War, Higginson was a captain in the 51st Massachusetts Volunteers. After sustaining an injury, he became colonel of the First South Carolina Volunteers, a regiment whose soldiers were former slaves. His experiences were recorded in *Army Life in a Black Regiment*.

Higginson was also greatly influenced by the transcendentalists. His own writing included essays about nature and spirituality. Later he would write about equality between the sexes. His writing was often featured in the *Atlantic Monthly*, a popular magazine. He wrote both fiction and nonfiction.

Higginson not only acted as a mentor to Dickinson, he also maintained a friendship with Helen Hunt Jackson and encouraged her in her writing career. He showed Jackson Dickinson's poetry, and thus fostered a friendship between the two women.

After Dickinson died, Higginson worked with Mabel Loomis Todd to edit Dickinson's first edition of poems for publication. He also wrote an article about his friendship with Dickinson in 1891 for the *Atlantic Monthly*. He died in 1911.

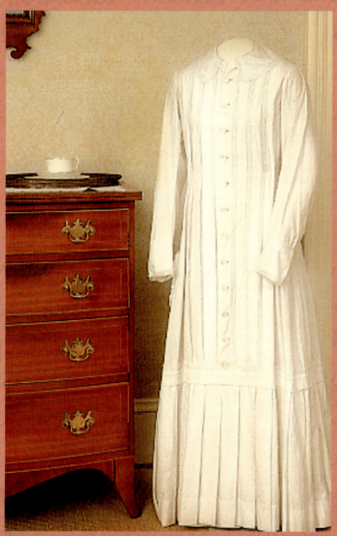

A white dress that Emily Dickinson wore is on display in the Dickinson's Homestead. Emily began wearing only white sometime around 1870.

# Chapter 7

## Challenges

In the 1860s, while she was in her thirties and the Civil War raged, Emily continued to write poetry in the confines of her home, and to help her mother with the housework. She became more and more dedicated to her garden, a beautiful space in the backyard in which she grew a number of both common and exotic flowers. She continued her long walks in the woods to collect specimens for her garden. Her niece, Martha Dickinson Bianchi, had this memory of Emily's handiwork: "There were carpets of lily-of-the-valley and pansies, platoons of sweet peas, hyacinths enough in May to give all the bees of summer dyspepsia. There were ribbons of peony hedges and rifts of daffodils in season, marigolds to distraction—a butterfly utopia."[1]

Emily's father added a conservatory on the house so that Emily could grow even more unusual and tropical plants that wouldn't have survived outside in the chilly New England winters. Among these, Emily grew a prize jasmine vine that Samuel Bowles had given her. She also forced bulbs, a method to get bulbs to bloom even if it isn't springtime. The bulbs are chilled and then put in a warm place, where they will bloom as if it were spring. Emily was able to enjoy the color and fragrance of her flowers year round. She loved both the wildflowers that grew abundantly in the fields and woods beyond her garden, and

# Chapter 7

likewise, the very exotic, difficult flowers that she had to fuss over in her conservatory. Her interests reflected the dual nature of Emily herself and of her poetry: at once simple—like the wildflowers—yet complex—like the tropical flowers.

Emily's garden provided an outdoor, private sanctuary where she could enjoy beauty and get fresh air yet still keep her solitude. She'd arrange her flowers into bouquets, which she'd send, often with poems attached. The flowers she grew also provided her with subjects for many of her poems. She assigned meaning to the different flowers to represent different ideals. According to Dickinson scholar Judith Farr: "The heliocentric daisy represented faithful devotion; the gentian, determination, ability, industry in the face of difficulty and scorn; the violet, modesty and fidelity; the lily, hallowed beauty."[2]

Dickinson studied the works of John Ruskin, an English writer and art critic. He especially defended and promoted landscape painters and discussed issues of art and writing. Specifically, he reacted against the industrial age and factory-made materials. He promoted the works of artists and craftspeople instead. He compared and contrasted how people approach the study of plants. Some study the different parts of a plant and classify it with the proper Latin terminology (as Emily had learned in

John Ruskin, an English writer and art critic, influenced Dickinson's writing.

school). Others, he argued, became emotionally attached to the plant. This was something that Dickinson understood as well.

Flowers were a way to mark the seasons. In the spring, Dickinson would praise and rejoice in the emergence of the bulbs after the long cold winter. The masses of crocus and daffodil blossoms represented hope and rebirth—and so had spiritual significance. Though she was uncertain of her own spiritual path, she found nature comforting. In the fall, when the frosts would kill some of her plants, she connected the destruction of winter to death that had indiscriminately taken away so many she had known and loved.

There is some speculation as to whether or not Dickinson suffered from Seasonal Affective Disorder, or SAD. This disorder is characterized by increased depression as the days grow shorter toward winter, then higher productivity and spirits as summer approaches. Evidence does point to Dickinson's preference for spring and summer. Just as many of her poems reveal the joy of the warmer seasons (and most of her poems were written during this time), some of her poems reveal her feelings about winter:

> There's a certain Slant of light,
> Winter Afternoons—
> That oppresses, like the Heft
> Of Cathedral Tunes.[3]

Was Dickinson suffering from SAD? Or did she merely prefer the seasons when she could be in her garden?

In 1863, Dickinson began to suffer from an eye ailment. She couldn't stand to be in bright light, and her eyes ached. She could no longer go outside during the day. She had to attend to her flowers in the early morning or at dusk, and she sometimes used a lantern while in the garden.

Leaving her home for the first time in many years, Dickinson traveled to Cambridge in April to November of 1864 and again in April to October of 1865 to seek treatment from Dr. Henry Willard Williams,

## Chapter 7

an ophthalmologist. Among other treatments, Dickinson was advised to avoid bright light, fine work, and reading. Being kept from the written word terrified her, as she considered reading one of her greatest solaces. The exact disease she had is unknown, though it is thought to have been anterior uveitis, an inflammation of the iris that causes light sensitivity and severe pain. Though she spent many months in Boston undergoing treatment, she most likely didn't spend much time socializing. She even referred to her time in Boston as prison or jail. At one point the doctor took away her pen, so she wrote with a pencil.

She was in exile from her beloved home, but Dickinson wasn't completely alone. She stayed at a boardinghouse with her cousins Louisa and Frances Norcross. The younger women loved watching and acting in dramatic productions, especially works of William Shakespeare. Their enthusiasm motivated Dickinson to read this classic English writer. In Amherst she started to read Shakespeare in earnest and seemed to like *Antony and Cleopatra*, a play about the ill-fated love affair between the Roman general Antony and the beautiful Egyptian queen Cleopatra.

When Dickinson returned from her second trip, she lost her dog, Carlo. She had relied on her canine companion to join her on walks through the countryside around Amherst. Also, that winter, Dickinson began to write less frequently than before.

In 1866, another child was born to Sue and Austin. Martha Dickinson grew to be a lively and social girl in this household of parties and important guests. In contrast, Emily grew more and more reclusive and spent less time at the Evergreens.

The Dickinson family continued to prosper. Edward's and Austin's law careers expanded, and Edward was successful at bringing another college to Amherst. In 1867, classes began at Massachusetts Agricultural College (now known as the University of Massachusetts at Amherst).

At or around 1870, Dickinson began wearing only white. When it happened is uncertain, though a poem from 1862 mentions a woman wearing white. Later, one of her dresses, made sometime in the late

*Challenges*

An early photograph of the Massachusetts Agricultural College in Amherst

1870s to early 1880s, was saved and is now on display in her house in Amherst. The color represents many things, and a number of people speculate as to why Dickinson wore white. It symbolizes simplicity and purity; however, there may have been a very practical reason for her decision. Dickinson wasn't one to follow fashion, so wearing white simplified her wardrobe.

During the 1870s, Dickinson still seemed to spend time with her family and interact with those in her circle of friends. Though she had already begun to grow reclusive, she wasn't as isolated as she would become later.

In 1870, Dickinson finally met Higginson in person. Because he had long been fascinated with Dickinson and her writing, he wrote about his meeting with her. He describes her as bringing him two day lilies as her introduction, "which she put in a childlike way into my hand, saying softly, under her breath, 'These are my introduction,' and adding, also, under her breath, in childlike fashion, 'Forgive me if I am frightened; I never see strangers and hardly know what I

## Chapter 7

say.'"[4] Higginson noted that Dickinson talked quite a bit that afternoon about her life and her family. She wondered how other people lived out in the real world. Higginson found the poet both fascinating and tiring. Her intensity wasn't easy for everyone for endure. He even noted, "The impression undoubtedly made on me was that of an excess of tension, and of something abnormal."[5]

Dickinson may have seemed strange to Higginson, but they remained friends. And Dickinson found that she needed her friends as she faced the future, which would bring many sad days.

# Cottage Gardens

Emily Dickinson wasn't the only one passionate about her flowers. During her lifetime, cottage gardens began around many New England homes. Traditionally, European gardens were formal, with organized rows of specific plants. Often, these gardens were very large and ornate. It was a different kind of garden than the humble cottage yard with an emphasis on hearty flowers—such as foxgloves, poppies, and daisies—medicinal herbs, vegetables, and fruiting trees. During the nineteenth century the division between the formal gardens of the rich and the simple gardens of the working class blurred. The practical cottage gardens of the working class were considered beautiful by the wealthier people, who began to emulate this informal style in bigger, more prosperous places. Designing cottage gardens became fashionable during the mid to late nineteenth century.

English gardeners William Robinson and later Gertrude Jekyll popularized the movement by creating and writing about gardens using the cottage style. The impressionist painter Claude Monet

A bright and colorful garden spills out behind and around a bench. Cottage gardens often include a place to sit and enjoy the flowers.

also had a spectacular garden with elements of the cottage style. He used his garden as a setting for many of his paintings.

Many Americans began imitating the British movement and designed cottage gardens of their own. These American gardens employed the same elements as their English counterparts. The cottage garden emphasized romantic flowering plants. The more abundant and informal, the better the garden.

Plants for the cottage garden include traditional and often highly fragrant flowers such as roses, lilies, and sweet peas. In addition, gardens usually include trellises, benches, herbs, and even vegetables. Some gardens had lawns for outdoor activities, while other gardens had a narrow path between mass plantings of flowers. The colors were mixed and the flowers were not kept back in borders but, rather, were left to spill out over the walkways. It is also a tradition have vegetables tucked in among the flowers. The cottage style is all at once beautiful, fragrant, and practical.

**Sweet pea**

A popular idea of the time was the language of flowers: Each flower represented an idea or emotion, so people could communicate their feelings through their choice of flowers. For example, roses represent love and pansies represent faithfulness and modesty. Such sentimental ideas could be presented in a bouquet, so the recipient could obtain not only the flowers, but also the idea behind them. The popularity of the language of flowers went well with the romantic cottage garden.

Gardening was a way for women to express themselves. This was a time when women didn't have the same opportunities that men did, and men didn't often have the opportunity to garden. Even with artistic expression, women's work was considered in-

Daylily

ferior. In the garden, however, women could express themselves with beautiful plants.

Gardening also took on a spiritual power. The nineteenth-century transcendentalist ideas worked well in the garden, where one could attribute the beauty of the plants to the powers of a higher being. Also, the garden's rebirth in spring and "death" in winter reflect the cycle of life. Even the spiritual idea of an afterlife is suggested as perennials and bulbs reawaken in spring.

For those with the money and time to do so, growing unusual plants or propagating (creating) new strains was also popular. Many who lived in cooler climates constructed conservatories in which they could grow exotic and tropical plants. In a time when traveling long distances could be very costly, creating the environment of another culture right at home was appealing. A tropical jungle in a cold New England house had a certain appeal.

Growing gardens and unique plants was not only a pleasurable activity, but it also proved to be a status symbol for many. In the same way that some people now compete over who has the nicest car or best electronic toys, some people in the nineteenth century competed over who had the best garden.

Cottage gardens are no longer as popular as they once were because they are time intensive. Also, because of modern supermarkets, most people no longer need to grow their own food. Yet cottage gardens still endure—even in some small suburban yards and on city rooftops.

A look inside the pantry at the Dickinson's Homestead, where Emily loved to bake. Among other treats, Emily made her famous gingerbread that was enjoyed by family and friends.

# Chapter 8

## Hiding Away

In the 1870s and 1880s, Emily grew increasingly reclusive. She wrote poems and letters and spent more and more time in the confines of her own home. She even stopped going to the Evergreens next door.

She continued to work in her beloved garden and still helped with the housework—especially because her mother's health had begun to deteriorate. Dickinson's baking skills were praised by her family. Her father liked Emily's bread the best and insisted that she be the one to make it. She was also applauded for her delicious cakes—she would use generous helpings of raisins and brandy in the batter. Her gingerbread was also very good, and a version of her recipe still survives. Albert Habegger notes that the recipe calls for "4 cups flour, ½ cup butter, ½ cup cream, a tablespoon of ginger, a teaspoon of soda, and salt, with molasses for sweetening."[1]

When she wasn't helping with the baking, Emily wrote more about memories and spent more time upstairs in her room. Sometimes, instead of meeting someone face to face, Dickinson would show her admiration by sending a poem or flowers. When the English writer Frances Hodgson Burnett visited Austin and Sue, she recalls receiving "a strange wonderful little poem lying on a bed of exquisite heartsease in a box."[2]

## Chapter 8

Frances Hodgson Burnett, a popular author, was often a guest at the Evergreens.

Though Dickinson hid when people came to the door, she did feel comfortable being around children. Often her niece Martha and nephew Ned would play with other neighborhood children around her house. She would work in the garden as the children played. Often she gave them treats. Either she would raid the pantry when the servant, Maggie, wasn't looking, or she would make her gingerbread and send it down in a basket. This could be a very dramatic moment if the children were playing some sort of game in which they pretended they were starving and lost or held prisoner somewhere. The children seemed delightful and imaginative to Dickinson. As a woman who was often described as childlike, she may have felt a kinship to these children.

Others around Dickinson were growing old and losing their health, which worried the poet greatly. In the 1870s, Edward Dickinson's health began to deteriorate. In June of 1874, while on a trip to protect railroad interests in Boston, Edward Dickinson had a stroke and died. The town of Amherst mourned the loss of a great leader, who had helped bring the modern world of railroads and higher education. The Dickinson family mourned the loss of their leader—especially Emily. Even though she was in her forties, her father had remained a very

Helen Hunt Jackson overcame tragedies to become an advocate for native people in California. She persuaded Dickinson to contribute a poem to a collection Jackson wanted to publish.

important person in her life. She grieved his death. He had been stern sometimes and didn't always share his daughter's taste for literature, but he had been the presence of stability at the Homestead.

Edward's death caused other problems among his children. As was the custom during that time, all of the family wealth and property went to the oldest son. However, since Edward didn't have a will when he died, there was some speculation as to how his wealth was supposed to be divided. This created friction between Vinnie and Austin. Emily's mother didn't have a say in the matter. Austin decided that

## Chapter 8

the three Dickinson women could stay at the Homestead and continue their lives as before.

At some point during the 1870s, Dickinson developed a friendship with Otis Phillips Lord, a judge on the Massachusetts Supreme Judicial Court. After Lord's wife died in 1877, the friendship between the judge and the poet grew to romance. Though Lord was closer to her father's age than to Emily's, they were both intelligent and thoughtful. They shared a love of literature and enjoyed time together. Letters went back and forth between the two.

Through Higginson, another friendship developed for Dickinson. This was with a woman who had grown up in Amherst but had since moved away. Helen Hunt Jackson was a writer as well, and the two writers began communicating through letters. Jackson was very different from Dickinson in many ways. She was a public figure and promoted her own writing in publications. She wanted to see Dickinson's poetry published. After coaxing Dickinson to offer a single poem for a collection of poetry, Dickinson finally agreed, and her poem "Success Is Counted Sweetest" was published in *A Masque of Poets* in 1878. This was one of Dickinson's few published poems during her lifetime. Jackson and Dickinson continued their friendship until Jackson's death in 1885.

# Helen Hunt Jackson

There was another writer who grew up in Amherst, and Dickinson had known her as a girl. This was Helen Hunt Jackson, who was born Helen Maria Fiske in 1830. Young Helen was boisterous and liked rough play. As she grew, she had to deal with a series of tragedies. Her mother died in 1844 and her father, who was a professor of language and philosophy at Amherst College, died in 1847.

She married Edward B. Hunt, an army captain who died in a military accident. She also lost both of her sons. Even after so many devastating experiences, Helen decided to earn her living by becoming a writer. She moved to Newport, Rhode Island, and met Thomas Wentworth Higginson, Dickinson's editor. He encouraged Helen in her writing, and she began to publish a number of works under various pseudonyms. It was during this time that Jackson and Dickinson corresponded and became reacquainted.

In 1873, Helen went to Colorado for her health. She most likely had tuberculosis and sought to live in a better climate. While she was there, she met William S. Jackson, a banker and railroad executive, whom she married in 1875.

Her 1876 novel *Mercy Philbrick's Choice* reportedly used Emily Dickinson as an inspiration for the main character. The novel is about a reclusive New England poet who decides not to remarry after her husband dies.

In 1879, after hearing a lecture by Chief Standing Bear, who discussed the plight of the Ponca Indians, Helen Hunt Jackson became an advocate for the native peoples who were being mistreated by the federal government. Her *A Century of Dishonor* was published in 1881 and was sent to all the members of Congress at Jackson's expense. It told of the mismanagement and mistreatment of the native peoples by the federal government. On the cover, Jackson had written the following message in red: "Look upon your hands: they are stained with the blood of your relations."[3] In the end, the book had little impact on changing the federal government's treatment of Native Americans.

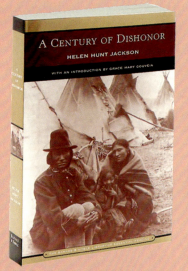

Helen Hunt Jackson's *A Century of Dishonor* described the terrible treatment endured by Native Americans.

Jackson then traveled to California and met Don Antonio Coronel, a man with extensive political experience, and learned about the plight of displaced Native Americans. When California became a part of the United States, the Native Americans were sent from the missions but could not reclaim their lands. This upset Jackson greatly, so she got the attention of the federal government—specifically, of the Commissioner of Indian Affairs, Hiram Price, who encouraged her to find out what she could about the conditions of the Native Americans in California. Jackson, along with Abbott Kinney, a businessman and writer, were appointed Special Commissioners to study the situation.

After a major investigation, Jackson completed a report in 1883. She wanted the federal government to help the native peoples by providing land for reservations and other assistance. Though the bill covering her recommendations passed in the U.S. Senate, it was defeated in the House of Representatives.

Jackson used the information from her investigation as a setting for a novel, *Ramona*, which became a bestseller. The book was a romance that revealed the mistreatment of a young Native American couple by racists. Jackson wrote with great energy, for she hoped the book would bring about change in the treatment of Native Americans the same way that Harriet Beecher Stowe's *Uncle Tom's Cabin* had changed people's views toward slavery. The impact was not as a great, however, because most readers were more caught up in the romantic elements of the story than with the plight of the Native Americans.

Chief Standing Bear lectured on the conditions of the Ponca Indians and moved Helen Hunt Jackson to help Native Americans.

In 1884, Jackson fell and broke her leg in Colorado. She went to California to recover and died there in 1885, apparently of cancer. After her death, Emily Dickinson sent a letter to Jackson's widower, William S. Jackson, declaring, "Helen of Troy will die, but Helen of Colorado, never."[4]

Emily's beloved nephew Thomas Gilbert Dickinson, or Gib, died of typhoid fever at the age of eight. The death of Gib caused great sorrow for Emily and the entire Dickinson family.

# Chapter 9

## Endings

The years following Edward's death were sorrowful. Emily's mother had a particularly hard time with the loss. On June 15, 1875, she suffered a stroke. The following year she broke her hip and required care from her daughters. In 1882, Emily Norcross Dickinson died. As a child and a young woman, Emily Dickinson had felt that her relationship with her mother was distant. In later years, when she took care of her aging mother, her feelings changed. This is revealed in a letter she wrote to her friend Elizabeth Holland: "We were never intimate . . . while she was our Mother—but Mines in the same Ground meet by tunneling and when she became our Child, the Affection came."[1] Dickinson had grown closer to her invalid mother when she began caring for her, just as her mother had once cared for her when she was young.

The years that followed were difficult ones for Dickinson, but, despite the illnesses and deaths of those around her, she kept her spirits up. It was an interesting contrast to the earlier years when she was outwardly social but inwardly suffering. Now, she seldom saw anyone outside her family and small group of friends, but she worked very hard at keeping cheerful. She also sent letters to others to keep their spirits up in times of hardship.

# Chapter 9

After her mother died and Emily no longer needed to care for her, Lord asked to marry him. She turned him down. She decided that she couldn't leave the house she had lived in and loved for so many years. She loved Lord dearly, but she felt too set in her ways at the Homestead.

In 1874, Austin and Sue's son Ned suffered from rheumatic fever and later from epileptic seizures and then more bouts with rheumatic fever. These illnesses most likely led to heart problems. Their concern for one son was followed by the joy of new life. In 1875, Thomas Gilbert was born to Susan and Austin. Gib, as he was called, grew to be a charming and intelligent young boy.

In 1877, Dickinson met with Bowles, who was suffering from overwork and stress, working both as an editor and as a social reformer. At first she didn't want to come downstairs and see him, but he insisted. She agreed and met with her friend. She created a poem from the result of their encounter: "A Word to a Friend." The poem touched Bowles deeply, and he wrote a letter to her, stating, "You are very good to like me so much and to say such sweet and encouraging things to me."[2]

The following year Bowles died. Emily sent words of comfort to Mary Bowles and others who mourned the loss of him, yet Emily herself was devastated. Judith Farr notes the following response from Dickinson: "She was probably the woman who was known to call his death an 'eclipse' since Bowles, with his eyes like 'comets' and his 'graphic countenance,' was her personal 'Sun.' "[3]

In 1881, Emily lost her friend Josiah Holland. Then in 1882, Charles Wadsworth also died. The loss of her parents and three other important people in her life couldn't have been easy for the poet.

Meanwhile, problems of a different kind started next door at the Evergreens. Austin met Mabel Loomis Todd, a beautiful and accomplished young woman who was the wife of a professor at Amherst College. Todd and Austin fell in love and began an extramarital affair. Despite the awkward circumstances, Todd was introduced to Dickinson's poetry and became a fan of her work. The two women exchanged

# Endings

letters and developed a friendship. Todd greatly admired the reclusive poet. At one point, she painted a picture of Indian pipes for Emily. The strange, rare flower, which grows in hidden dark places, seemed to symbolize her friend. Dickinson thanked Todd: "That without suspecting it you should send me the preferred flower of life, seems almost supernatural, and the sweet glee that I felt at meeting it, I could confide to none."[4]

In 1883, Dickinson's beloved nephew Gib contracted typhoid fever and died. He was only eight years old. Gib's death had a profound effect on Emily. She went to the Evergreens to visit the grieving family (the first time in about fifteen years). There, the smell of the disinfectant in the house made Dickinson ill herself. She remained sick for some time after Gib's death. Despite her own illness, she still managed to send hopeful messages to her family and friends to keep their strength up.

In 1885, while making a cake with her servant Martha, Dickinson fainted and remained unconscious for the rest of the day. In the months that followed she had many fainting and dizzy spells. In November she was sick again. The following spring she seemed to be doing better, but she sent a strange and prophetic note to her cousins Frances and Louisa:

"Little Cousins,
Called back.
Emily."[5]

The phrase *called back* comes from a novel popular at the time by Hugh Conway that is about a blind man who witnesses a murder. He later gains telepathic powers, which he uses to find the murderer. Like the character, Emily had a sense of something unforeseen. She senses that she will be "called back" in death.

On May 13, 1886, Dickinson reportedly suffered from a stroke. She lost consciousness and stayed that way until May 15 when she took her last breath. At age fifty-five, Emily Dickinson was dead. In the official

## Chapter 9

records Dickinson died of Bright's disease, a class of illnesses that affect the kidneys, yet Dr. Norbert Hirschhorn and Polly Longsworth argue that Dickinson probably died of severe primary hypertension, a type of heart disease. The symptoms of her illness and appearance didn't match the characteristics associated with kidney disease. Hypertension seems plausible for a number of other reasons as well. As Dickinson biographer Alfred Habegger notes: "[T]he stress under which the poet lived; the emotional effects of her bereavements [the deaths of those close to her]; the state of medical science at the time; and the record of symptoms in her last two and a half years"[6] point to the possibility of hypertension rather than Bright's disease.

Whatever the cause of Emily's death, Austin and Vinnie were devastated. Their sister's presence had been an important part of their daily lives. Their source of comfort was gone.

The funeral was held in the library of the Homestead. According to Judith Farr, it was a beautiful day where "birds sang full-throated outside the windows and butterflies flitted among her richly colored flowers."[7] Those in attendance, many of whom hadn't seen Dickinson in years, were surprised at how young she looked in her casket. Apparently her hair wasn't gray and her face was still smooth, like that of a younger woman. Lavinia put flowers in her sister's coffin. She placed heliotrope, lady's slippers, and blue violets, since Emily had loved these flowers so much. The poem "No Coward Soul Is Mine" by Emily Brontë was read—a poem that Dickinson greatly admired. Certainly, like the Brontë sisters, Dickinson had known what it was like to endure hardships but stay courageous.

After the ceremony, Farr reported, "Dickinson had asked to have her coffin not driven but carried through fields of buttercups to the West cemetery, always in sight of the house."[8] She was buried near her parents in the Dickinson family plot.

# The Brontë Sisters

Living in England in the middle of the nineteenth century, a trio of sisters in need of money began writing poetry and novels. Charlotte, Emily, and Anne Brontë grew up with three other siblings in Haworth, England. Their father was a clergyman, and their mother died when they were young. Their aunt, Elizabeth Branwell, came to help raise the children, but she was cold and detached from them.

The four eldest daughters—Maria, Elizabeth, Charlotte, and Emily—were sent to a boarding school called Cowan Bridge. The school was horrible. The students were treated cruelly and the food and living conditions were substandard. As a result, the two oldest Brontë daughters—Maria and Elizabeth—died of typhoid fever and tuberculosis, diseases most probably brought on by the conditions in the school. They were only ten and eleven years old. Charlotte and Emily were taken home to join their brother, Branwell, and their younger sister, Anne. Saddened by the death of their older siblings, they sought comfort in each other's company. They continued their education at home, spending many hours reading and creating the imaginary worlds of "Angria" and "Gondal."

Later, Charlotte went away to school again. This time her experience was much better. She continued at the school as a teacher, which she didn't enjoy as much as being a student. Eventually, Charlotte and Emily were sent off to finishing school in Brussels. Charlotte fell in love with the owner of the school, but he was married, older, and didn't return her feelings. After schooling, the sisters found work as governesses and found it very dissatisfying and demeaning; however, they had to keep their jobs, as Branwell had become an alcohol and opium addict and was unable to provide for the family.

Charlotte and Emily considered starting a school of their own, but they couldn't get enough people interested in attending. Finally, after reading some of her sister Emily's poems, Charlotte decided that the three girls could make a living by writing. Since female writers were not always taken seriously during that time,

**A portrait of Anne, Emily, and Charlotte Brontë painted by their brother, Patrick Branwell Brontë.**

and the Brontë sisters wished to remain anonymous, the three used the names Currer, Ellis, and Acton Bell to replace Charlotte, Emily, and Anne Brontë.

Their first book, a collection of poems, didn't do very well. The three sisters refused to give up; they began writing novels, and these did better. The first novels published were Emily's

*Wuthering Heights* and Anne's *Agnes Grey*, followed by Charlotte's *Jane Eyre*. The novels established the sisters as writers (though there was a great deal of speculation as to who the "Bell siblings" were.) *Jane Eyre* received the most praise.

Though the novels reflected other sentimental books of the era, the Brontës' work stood out because each novel had a strong female character. In *Jane Eyre*, Charlotte Brontë integrated elements from her own life. The school Jane attends is not unlike Cowan Bridge, and plain and practical Jane was similar to Charlotte as well.

Other novels followed, including Charlotte's *Shirley* and *Villette*. Many critics commented that women couldn't write novels as insightful and good as these novels were.

The Brontë sisters were starting to make a name for themselves when tragedy struck. Their beloved Branwell died of an illness, perhaps tuberculosis or bronchitis, as a result of his alcohol and opium dependency. At the funeral, Emily caught a cold and developed tuberculosis. Anne contracted the sickness as well, and both Emily and Anne died in 1848.

Charlotte's identity was at last revealed, and she went on to be a part of the literary crowd in London. Her sadness over her recent losses was difficult to overcome, but in 1854, Charlotte married Arthur Bell Nicholls and seemed happy. However, after she became pregnant, she became very ill. She died in March 1855, possibly of complications in her pregnancy or perhaps from tuberculosis.

The Brontë sisters lived short and tragic lives, but the impact of their writing is still felt today. They influenced a number of writers in their time—including Emily Dickinson. They also paved the way for future women writers and strong female characters.

A close-up look at Emily Dickinson's headstone. It is inscribed with her date of birth, the phrase *called back*, and the date of her death.

The Dickinson family plot in Amherst, Massachusetts, is where Emily and the rest of her family are buried.

# Chapter 10

## The Legacy

Vinnie stood before Emily's cherry wood cabinet. She was carrying out her sister's wish to destroy her letters and papers. When she opened the drawer, she found something she wasn't expecting—the hand-sewn books of paper containing pages and pages of Emily's poems. She also found countless scraps of paper—shopping lists and envelopes—on which were written many more poems. In all, she found over seventeen hundred. Though Vinnie did destroy her sister's letter collection, she couldn't bring herself to burn the poems. There was something very special about these, and Vinnie couldn't let them go. She had no idea at the time that her decision not to grant her sister's wish would be the greatest gift she could give to the world—a chance to glimpse into the very private but very large world of Emily Dickinson.

After Vinnie found Emily's poems, she gave them to Sue Dickinson to edit and publish. Even though Sue had admired Dickinson's work during her lifetime, for some reason she didn't make an effort to get them published after Emily's death. Losing patience with Sue, Vinnie turned to Mabel Loomis Todd, who put together the collection. She is the one who named Dickinson's handmade books fascicles, meaning "little bunches of flowers." She enlisted Higginson to help with the editing.

## Chapter 10

In 1890 a collection of the poems was published and enthusiastically received. *Poems by Emily Dickinson* did very well. Some people didn't fully understand Dickinson's work and felt that the lack of adherence to standard poetry and punctuation made her poems substandard to other poets' work. But many saw that she had a gift that transcended the standards of the time. Todd published a second series of poems in 1891, and a third in 1896.

In 1891, in a review in *Harper's New Monthly Magazine*, the writer notes that Dickinson's poems are short, but complete: "They are each a compassed whole, a sharply finished point, and there is evidence, circumstantial and direct, that the author spared no pains in the perfect expression of her ideals."[1] The reviewer continued, "If nothing else had come out of our life but this strange poetry we should feel that in the work of Emily Dickinson America, or new England rather, had made a distinctive addition to the literature of the world, and could not be left out of any record of it."[2]

In 1924, Sue's daughter, Martha Dickinson Bianchi, published an edition of Emily's poems. She and Mabel Loomis Todd's daughter, Millicent Todd Bingham, also wrote books about Dickinson's life and work. These two women kept Dickinson's popularity alive.

Later, in the 1950s, editors reexamined the original texts of Dickinson's poems. Since the collections published in the 1890s had been edited, and consequently the poems had been altered, care was taken to publish Dickinson's poems in their original format, with her original use of dashes. Dickinson's poetry has continued to be very popular. She is considered one the most important poets of nineteenth-century America. Her work has been translated into many languages.

But it isn't just Dickinson's poetry that continues to interest us, it is her life as well. In Amherst, Massachusetts, the Homestead and the Evergreens are open to the public as part of the Emily Dickinson Museum, which is owned by Amherst College. During the year the museum hosts many events, including poetry readings and walks through the gardens. Tours allow people to see many of the rooms in the house, including Dickinson's bedroom, where she wrote her poems.

# The Legacy

Amherst College and the Mount Holyoke Female Seminary (now Mount Holyoke College) still exist. So do a number of the houses and churches in Amherst that had significance for Dickinson. There has even been a movement to get the town's name changed from Amherst to Emily. Letters and poems that Dickinson wrote are kept in libraries there. The herbarium Dickinson created as an adolescent is kept in the Emily Dickinson Room in the Houghton Rare Book Library at Harvard University in Cambridge, Massachusetts.

For those interested, there are many professional organizations dedicated exclusively to the study of the poet's work, including the Emily Dickinson International Society. Scholars continue to create books and web sites about Dickinson and her poetry even today; there is always a new way to look at the poet's work.

In 2002, a film was released called *Loaded Gun: Life and Death and Dickinson*. It explores why Dickinson is still popular. Without making any clear conclusions, the film looks at the many roles that Dickinson had and the impact of her poetry on popular culture.

Because Dickinson's fame is so widespread, some people have taken advantage of it. In the 1980s, a man skilled in forgery, Mark Hofmann, wrote a poem that looked very much like one Dickinson would have written. This was one of many forgeries Hofmann created. He used the same kind of paper that some

From the 2002 film *Loaded Gun: Life and Death and Dickinson*

## Chapter 10

of her poems were on, and the handwriting was very similar to hers. In addition, the poem was about nature and God—themes that were used by Dickinson.

Unfortunately, Hofmann didn't stop at forgery. He was also convicted of murder. It was after he was in prison for murder, in 1997, when the forged poem showed up as an auction piece and was purchased by Jones Library in Amherst for over twenty thousand dollars. It was only after someone decided to do some research on some of the details in the poem that they figured out it was a forgery by Hofmann.

Some scholars still hope that some lost poem, letter, or other clue to Emily's life will show up. Many still want to find out more about this elusive poet's life.

After more than 150 years, why does Dickinson still move us? She managed to reach across time by conveying her thoughts and feelings in a way we understand. The joy of life, the loss of love, the fear of death, the appreciation of nature—these are all intrinsic parts of who we are.

# Emily on Ebay

In April 2000, Philip F. Gura, a professor of American literature and culture and collector of early photography, made an astonishing find on eBay, an online auction site. He saw the description "Vintage Emily Dickinson Albumen Photo" and laughed, but curiosity caused him to click on the description to see the photo. He was sure that the seller must not have known that the only known photographic image of Dickinson was the daguerreotype taken of her when she was an adolescent.

Ebay began in 1995 and is now a highly successful auction web site, where people buy and sell a wide variety of items. Items are sold after bids are placed. The highest bidder gets to buy the item.

Gura was surprised to see that the image of the photograph on eBay did look unexpectedly like an older version of the young woman in the known daguerreotype. Over the next couple of weeks, he bid and won the picture for $481.00. It was a risk, because there was really no evidence that another picture existed.

When the photo arrived, Gura was delighted to see that the image looked genuine. On the back of the photo, he found the words *Emily Dickinson died Dec 1886* (which isn't precisely correct since Dickinson died in May of 1886). Then the real work began. After being inundated by calls from reporters, Gura contacted several people who could analyze the photograph. He found that the photo he had purchased was an albumen copy, made in the 1860s, of an earlier daguerreotype (made between 1839 and 1857, when daguerreotype was popular).

By doing an analysis of the dress the woman is wearing in the picture, historians of costumes dated the fashion to be somewhere between 1848 and 1853. This would fit into the time when Emily was in her late teens to early twenties, and matched the image of the woman in the photo.

Philip F. Gura discovered this picture on eBay and, taking a risk, purchased it. Is it Emily Dickinson? After an extensive investigation, experts agree that it could possibly be an image of the poet.

Professor Richard Jantz and a student of the Forensic Anthropology Center at the University of Tennessee then analyzed the print and compared it to the known daguerreotype of Dickinson. The results showed that the placement of certain features such as the eyes and the distance between the nose and mouth in both photographs provided strong evidence that the second photograph could indeed be Dickinson at a later age.

Looking at biographical evidence, we know that when the original known image of Dickinson was made, she was a teen and getting over an illness—perhaps even showing signs of tuberculosis. The second image would have been made when Dickinson had recovered and gained back some weight. This would explain why her face looks fuller in the second photo.

So why was this second photo not mentioned or kept by family members? Gura and a biographer of Dickinson's work, Alfred Habegger, speculate that Dickinson could have had the photo made, and then given it to Charles Wadsworth. If Wadsworth had the photo, it could have been hidden by his family, who didn't like the rumors about a potential romantic relationship between him and Dickinson. But this idea is still speculation.

There is also some evidence that the copy of the photo belonged to Charles Clark, a friend of both Dickinson and Wadsworth. Clark, who began a correspondence with Dickinson in the 1880s, had handwriting similar to that found on the back of the photo. Again, there is only a similarity, which isn't proof that the writing is indeed his.

The question still remains: Is the second photo a newfound image of Dickinson? Or is it a forgery? Or is it an image of someone else completely? Once, in a letter to Higginson, she replied to his request for a picture by stating that she didn't have a picture now. Though scholars have traditionally thought this was proof that another image of Dickinson didn't exist, the letter is being reexamined. She may have had the second photograph and then given it away—she wouldn't have had it "now."

Strong evidence reveals that the picture may indeed be of the poet, but there isn't solid proof. Meanwhile, scholars will continue to consider the possibility. Another copy of the photograph may eventually show up, or a letter might be found with the right evidence to end this mystery. Professor Gura may have stumbled across a great find; he may own the only other known photographic image of the poet—and he found it on eBay.

# Chronology

**1830**   Emily Elizabeth Dickinson is born on December 10 in Amherst, Massachusetts.

**1840**   Emily begins school at Amherst Academy. The Dickinson family moves to a house on North Pleasant Street.

**1844**   Emily travels to Boston.

**1846**   Emily stays with her Aunt Lavinia to recover her mental and physical health.

**1847**   Emily enters Mount Holyoke Female Seminary.

**1850**   Dickinson's witty valentine is published in *The Indicator*.

**1855**   Dickinson travels to Washington, D.C., and Philadelphia.

**1856**   Austin Dickinson and Susan Gilbert get married.

**1855**   Dickinson experiences an unknown emotional crisis and begins creating books of her poems.

**1862**   After reading the article "A Letter to a Young Contributor," Dickinson sends four of her poems to Thomas Wentworth Higginson.

**1864**   Dickinson travels to Cambridge twice for eye treatment.

**1870**   Dickinson meets Higginson for the first time.

**1873**   Father, Edward Dickinson, dies.

**1878**   Emily agrees to publish "Success Is Counted Sweetest" in a poetry anthology.

**1882**   Mother, Emily Norcross Dickinson, dies.

**1883**   Nephew Thomas Gilbert Dickinson, age eight, dies.

**1886**   Emily Elizabeth Dickinson dies on May 15.

# Selected Works

## Poems
The first lines (and titles) of some of Emily Dickinson's most popular poems, with the year each was written.

*After great pain, a formal feeling comes* (1862)
*All overgrown by cunning moss* (1860)
*A narrow Fellow in the Grass* (1865)
*A wounded dear—leaps highest* (1860)
*Because I could not stop for death* (1862)
*I died for Beauty—but it was scarce* (1862)
*I dwell in Possibility—* (1862)
*I felt a Cleaving in my Mind* (1864)
*I have no Life but this* (1877)
*I heard a Fly buzz—when I died* (1863)
*I like to see it lap the Miles* (1862)
*I'm Nobody! Who are you?* (1861)
*I never saw a Moor* (1864)
*It will be Summer—eventually* (1862)
*My Life had stood—a Loaded Gun* (1863)
*The Soul selects her own Society* (1862)
*There's a certain Slant of light* (1862)
*There's been a Death, in the Opposite House* (1863)
*This is my letter to the World* (1863)
*This was a Poet* (1862)
*Safe in their Alabaster Chambers* (1859)

## Books
*The Complete Poems of Emily Dickinson*, ed. Thomas H. Johnson (Boston: Little Brown & Co., 1960).
*The Letters of Emily Dickinson*, ed. Thomas H. Johnson and Theodora Ward (Cambridge, MA: The Belknap Press of Harvard University Press, 1958).

# Timeline in History

| | |
|---|---|
| **1770** | The British poet William Wordsworth is born. |
| **1775–1776** | Thomas Jefferson writes a draft of the Declaration of Independence. |
| **1796** | Edward Jenner develops the smallpox vaccination. |
| **1800** | The haiku becomes a popular form of poetry in Japan. |
| **1836** | Ralph Waldo Emerson's essay "Nature" is published. |
| **1845–1850** | The potato blight causes the Great Famine in Ireland. |
| **1847** | *Wuthering Heights* and *Jane Eyre* are published. |
| **1848** | E.B. Hitchcock names *Anomoepus intermedius*, a dinosaur known only from its tail print. |
| **1857** | Elizabeth Barrett Browning's *Aurora Leigh* is published. |
| **1859** | Charles Darwin's *Origin of the Species* is published, and the debate over evolution begins. |
| **1861–1865** | The Civil War is fought in the United States. |
| **1865** | The Thirteenth Amendment is ratified in Congress; slavery ends in the United States. |
| **1876** | Alexander Graham Bell patents the telephone. |
| **1884** | Mark Twain's novel *The Adventures of Huckleberry Finn* is published. |
| **1900** | Kodak sells a Brownie camera for personal use. |
| **1910** | Hallmark begins printing greeting cards. |
| **1914–1918** | World War One is waged. |
| **1920** | The Nineteenth Amendment to the Constitution is passed; women earn the right to vote. |
| **1931** | The word game Scrabble is invented. |
| **1939–1945** | World War II is waged. |

# Chapter Notes

**Chapter 1**
**In a House in Amherst**
1. Emily Dickinson, *The Poems of Emily Dickinson* (Cambridge, Massachusetts: The Belknap Press of Harvard University Press, 2005), p. 235.
2. Ibid., p. 342.

**Chapter 2**
**Growing Up with Life and Death**
1. Emily Dickinson, qtd. in Alfred Habegger, *My Wars Are Laid Away in Books: The Life of Emily Dickinson* (New York: Random House, 2001), p. 92.

**Chapter 3**
**Studying Nature**
1. Emily Dickinson, *The Poems of Emily Dickinson* (Cambridge, Massachusetts: The Belknap Press of Harvard University Press, 2005), p. 513.
2. Ibid., p. 17.
3. Emily Dickinson, qtd. in Alfred Habegger, *My Wars Are Laid Away in Books: The Life of Emily Dickinson* (New York: Random House, 2001), pp. 154–155.
4. Dickinson, pp. 39–40.

5. Ibid., p. 549.
6. Daniel T. Fiske, qtd. in Habegger, p. 152.
7. Paul Crumbly, "Emily Dickinson's Life," *Modern American Poetry*, http://www.english.uiuc.edu/maps/poets/a_f/dickinson/bio.htm.
8. Emily Dickinson, qtd. in Habegger, p. 173.
9. Emily Dickinson, *The Poems of Emily Dickinson*, p. 219.
10. Emily Dickinson, qtd. in Habegger, p. 179.
11. Thomas Wentworth Higginson, "Emily Dickinson's Letters" *The Atlantic Monthly*, October 1891, p. 447.

**Chapter 4**
**Away from Home and Back Again**
1. "Mary Lyon," Mount Holyoke College, http://www.mtholyoke.edu/marylyon/
2. Emily Dickinson, *Letters of Emily Dickinson*, edited by Mabel Loomis Todd (Cleveland, Ohio: The World Publishing Company, 1951), p. 24.
3. Ibid., p. 39.
4. Ibid., p. 225.

5. Paul Crumbly, "Emily Dickinson's Life," *Modern American Poetry*, http://www.english.uiuc.edu/maps/poets/a_f/dickinson/bio.htm

6. Emily Dickinson, *The Poems of Emily Dickinson* (Cambridge, Massachusetts: The Belknap Press of Harvard University Press, 2005), p. 73.

7. Judith Farr, *The Gardens of Emily Dickinson* (Cambridge, Massachusetts: Harvard University Press, 2004), p. 30.

**Chapter 5**
**Emily, the Poet**

1. Emily Dickinson, *The Poems of Emily Dickinson* (Cambridge, Massachusetts: The Belknap Press of Harvard University Press, 2005), p. 15

2. Emily Dickinson, *Letters of Emily Dickinson*, edited by Mabel Loomis Todd (Cleveland, Ohio: The World Publishing Company, 1951), p. 87.

3. Emily Dickinson, *The Poems of Emily Dickinson*, p. 176.

4. Emily Dickinson, qtd. in Alfred Habegger, *My Wars Are Laid Away in Books: The Life of Emily Dickinson* (New York: Random House, 2001), p. 350.

5. Ibid., p. 351.

6. Habegger, p. 355.

**Chapter 6**
**The Literary Life**

1. Elizabeth Barrett Browning, qtd. in Alfred Habegger, *My Wars Are Laid Away in Books: The Life of Emily Dickinson* (New York, Random House, 2001), p. 386.

2. Emily Dickinson, *The Poems of Emily Dickinson* (Cambridge, Massachusetts: The Belknap Press of Harvard University Press, 2005), p. 64.

3. Thomas Wentworth Higginson, "Letter to a Young Contributor," Dickinson Electronic Archives, http://www.emilydickinson.org/higgyc/yct1.html

4. Thomas Wentworth Higginson, "Emily Dickinson's Letters," *The Atlantic Monthly*, October, 1891, p. 446.

5. Ibid.

6. Ibid., p. 447.

7. Ibid.

**Chapter 7**
**Challenges**

1. Martha Dickinson Bianchi, qtd. in Judith Farr, *The Gardens of Emily Dickinson* (Cambridge,

Massachusetts: Harvard University Press, 2004), p. 219.

2. Judith Farr, *The Gardens of Emily Dickinson* (Cambridge, Massachusetts: Harvard University Press 2004) p. 191.

3. Emily Dickinson, *The Poems of Emily Dickinson* (Cambridge, Massachusetts: The Belknap Press of Harvard University Press, 2005), p. 142.

4. Thomas Wentworth Higginson, "Emily Dickinson's Letters," *The Atlantic Monthly*, October 1891, p. 452.

5. Thomas Wentworth Higginson, qtd. in Alfred Habegger, *My Wars are Laid Away in Books: The Life of Emily Dickinson* (New York: Random House, 2001), p. 524.

## Chapter 8
## Hiding Away

1. Alfred Habegger, *My Wars Are Laid Away in Books: The Life of Emily Dickinson* (New York: Random House, 2001), pp. 502–503.

2. Frances Hodgson Burnett, qtd. in Habegger, p. 541.

3. Helen Hunt Jackson, Historical Society of Southern California, http://www.socalhistory.org/Biographies/hhjackson.htm.

4. Emily Dickinson, qtd. in Habegger, p. 625.

## Chapter 9
## Endings

1. Emily Dickinson, qtd. in Alfred Habegger, *My Wars Are Laid Away in Books: The Life of Emily Dickinson* (New York: Random House, 2001), p. 607.

2. Ibid., p. 572.

3. Judith Farr, *The Gardens of Emily Dickinson* (Cambridge, Massachusetts: Harvard University Press, 2004), p. 36.

4. Ibid., p. 15.

5. Emily Dickinson, qtd. in Habegger, p. 625.

6. Habegger, p. 623.

7. Farr, pp. 2–3.

8. Ibid., p. 3.

## Chapter 10
## The Legacy

1. *Harper's New Monthly Magazine*, January 1891, vol. 82, issue 488, p. 320.

2. Ibid.

# Further Reading

**For Young Adults**

Bloom, Harold. *Emily Dickinson*. New York: Chelsea House Publishers, 1999.

Borus, Audrey. *A Student's Guide to Emily Dickinson*. Berkeley Heights, New Jersey: Enslow Publishers, 2005.

Janeczko, Paul B. *Seeing the Blue Between: Advice and Inspiration for Young Poets*. Cambridge, Massachusetts: Candlewick Press, 2002.

Macdonald, Fiona. *Women in 19th-Century America*. New York: Peter Bedrick Books, 2001.

**Works Consulted**

Amherst College Geology, "Department History." http://www.amherst.edu/~geology/dept_history/

Collins, Gail. *America's Women: 400 Years of Dolls, Drudges, Helpmates, and Heroines*. New York: William Morrow, 2003.

"Division of Tuberculosis Elimination," Centers for Disease Control and Prevention. http://www.cdc.gov/nchstp/tb/default.htm

Farr, Judith. *The Gardens of Emily Dickinson*. Cambridge, Massachusetts: Harvard University Press, 2004.

Gordon, Lyndall. *Charlotte Brontë: A Passionate Life*. New York: W. W. Norton & Company, 1994.

Gura, Philip. F. "How I Met and Dated Miss Emily Dickinson: An Adventure on eBay." Common-Place. January 2004. http://www.common-place.org/vol-04/no-02/gura/

Habegger, Alfred. *My Wars Are Laid Away in Books: The Life of Emily Dickinson*. New York: Random House, 2001.

*Harper's New Monthly Magazine*. January 1891, vol. 82, issue 488.

Historical Society of Southern California. "Helen Hunt Jackson." http://www.socialhistory.org/Biographies/hhjackson.htm

Kazin, Alfred. *God and the American Writer*. New York: Alfred A. Knopf, 1997.

*Letters of Emily Dickinson*. Edited by Mabel Loomis Todd. Cleveland, Ohio: The World Publishing Company, 1951.

Lloyd, Christopher, and Richard Bird. *The Cottage Garden*. New York: Prentice Hall, 1990.

"Mary Lyon" Mount Holyoke College. http://www.mtholyoke.edu/marylyon/

Nina Baym, General Editor. *The Norton Anthology of American Literature: Shorter Version*, Sixth Edition. New York: Norton & Co, 2003.

McDermott, John. F. M.D. "Emily Dickinson Revisited: A Study of Periodicity in Her Work." *The American Journal of Psychiatry*, May 2001. http://ajp.psychiatryonline.org/cgi/content/full/158/5/686

Reuben, Paul. "Early Nineteenth Century—American Transcendentalism: A Brief Introduction." *PAL: Perspectives in American Literature.* CSU Stanislaus. http://www.csustan.edu/english/reuben/pal/chap4/4intro.html

Sanderson, Richard. "Edward Hitchcock: Stargazer and Astronomer." http://www.reflector.org/stargaze/hitchcoc/hitchcoc.htm

Sarrel, Mathew. "A History of Tuberculosis," New Jersey Department of Health and Senior Services. http://www.state.nj.us/health/cd/tbhistry.htm

*The Web of American Transcendentalism*. Virginia Commonwealth University. http://www.vcu.edu/engweb/transcendentalism/

Van Ophen, Marieke. *From Revolution to Reconstruction.* "The Iron Horse: The impact of Railroads on 19th-Century American Society." http://www.let.rug.nl/~usa/E/ironhorse/ironhorsexx.htm

Walker, Herbert T. *The Evolution of the American Locomotive*. http://www.catskillarchive.com/rrextra/absa1.Html

Worrall, Simon. "The Impersonation of Emily." *Guardian Unlimited*. April 8, 2000. http://books.guardian.co.uk/departments/poetry/story/0,6000,156998,00.html

**On the Internet**

American Transcendentalism Web
http://www.vcu.edu/engweb/transcendentalism/

Dickinson Electronic Archives
http://www.emilydickinson.org/

Emily Dickinson International Society
http://www.case.edu/affil/edis/edisindex.html

Emily Dickinson Museum
http://www.emilydickinsonmuseum.org/

Modern American Poetry: Emily Dickinson
http://www.english.uiuc.edu/maps/poets/a_f/dickinson/dickinson.htm

# Glossary

**abolition** (aa-buh-LIH-shun) The act of getting rid of a system or ending a practice, especially slavery.

**auspices** (OS-pih-sez) Friendly patronage or guidance.

**conservatory** (kun-SER-vah-tor-ee) A structure, made partially or entirely of glass, in which plants are grown. It is usually attached to a house.

**daguerreotype** (duh-GEH-roh-typ) The first practical and commercial photographic process, invented by Louis Daguerre.

**dyspepsia** (dis-PEP-shuh) Indigestion, upset stomach, or ill humor.

**eradicate** (ih-RAA-dih-kayt) To do away with completely.

**extramarital** (ek-struh-MAA-rih-tul) Describing a relationship between a married person and someone other than his or her spouse.

**fascicles** (FAA-sih-kuls) A small or slender bundle; also, one of the divisions of a book published in parts.

**haiku** (hye-KOO) a Japanese verse form of three lines, the first and last lines usually containing five syllables and the middle line containing seven syllables.

**heliocentric** (hee-lee-oh-SEN-trik) Sun-centered or relating to the sun as the center.

**literary** (LIH-tuh-rayr-ee) Of or relating to literature or writing.

**ophthalmologist** (off-thuh-MAH-luh-jist) A physician who specializes in the treatment of eye diseases.

**rationalism** (RAA-shuh-nuh-lism) The reliance on reason for the basis of religious belief.

**reclusive** (re-KLOO-siv) Shut in or solitary.

**cupola** (KYOO-puh-luh) A structure built on the top of a roof.

**stanza** (STAN-zah) A unit, part, or fixed number of lines in a poem.

**sonnet** (SAH-net) A fixed verse form usually containing fourteen lines.

# Index

*American Journal of Science*  31
Amherst Academy  25–30, 93
   Amherst College  26, 31, 33, 92, 93
Amherst, Massachusetts  8, 15–16, 46, 90, 93
Arch Street Presbyterian Church  48
*Atlantic Monthly*  63, 65
Aurora Leigh  56
Bianchi, Martha Dickinson (niece)  37, 65, 68, 71, 76, 92
Bingham, Millicent Todd (daughter of Mabel Loomis)  92
Blackwell, Henry  63
Bowdoin, Elbridge  45–46
Bowles, Mary  55, 84
Bowles, Samuel  55–56, 57, 84
Branwell, Elizabeth  87
Brehmer, Hermann  22
   Bright's disease  86
Brontë, Anne  56, 87–89
Brontë, Charlotte  39, 56, 87–89
Brontë, Emily  36, 86, 87–89
Brontë, Patrick Branwell  87–89
Brown, John (Harpers Ferry)  61–62
Browning, Robert, and Elizabeth Barrett  39, 56
Burnett, Frances Hodgson  7, 75–76
Burns, Anthony  63

Civil War  57, 61, 63, 65
Clark, Charles  96
Congregational Church  8, 18
Conway, Hugh  86
Coronel, Antonio  80
Daguerre, Louis  29
Dickinson, Edward (father)  15–16, 17, 18, 47, 49, 68, 76–77
Dickinson, William Austin  7, 15, 27, 47, 48, 49, 58, 68, 75, 78, 84–85, 86
Dickinson, Edward "Ned" (nephew)  58, 76, 84
Dickinson, Emily
   ancestors of  15–16, 17
   and baking  37, 74, 75, 76
   birth of  15
   clothing of  64, 68–69
   death of  85, 86, 90
   education of  19, 25–28, 35–37
   emotional breakdown of  50, 58–59
   eye problems  67–68
   health of  26, 27, 28, 37, 40, 49, 67, 85
   images of  29–30, 34, 54, 95–97
   and plants  24, 25–26, 27, 65–66, 67, 75, 85, 86
   poems of  10, 26–28, 40, 45–46, 47, 56, 58–60, 66, 67, 84, 91

Dickinson, Emily Norcross (mother)   15–16, 18, 19, 49, 78, 83
Dickinson, Lavinia Norcross (sister)   15, 47–48, 78, 86, 91
Dickinson, Lucretia Gunn   16, 17
Dickinson, Nathaniel, and Ann Gull   15–16
Dickinson, Samuel Fowler   6, 16, 18, 58–59
Dickinson, Thomas Gilbert (nephew)   82, 84, 85
Diesel, Rudolph   53
Eliot, George (Marian Evans)   57
Emerson, Ralph Waldo   8, 38, 42, 55
Emmons, Henry Vaughan   38
Evergreens   7–8, 48, 50, 68, 85, 92
Farr, Judith   68, 87
Fiske, Rev. Daniel T.   27
Frost, Robert   12
Gilbert, Martha   47
Gilbert, Susan (m. Austin Dickinson)   7–8, 44, 47–50, 85, 91
Ginsberg, Allen   13
Graves, John Long   47
Gura, Philip F.   95–97
Haiku   13
Habegger, Albert   51, 77, 86, 96
Harpers Ferry, Virginia   64
Harte, Bret   7, 48

Hawthorne, Nathaniel   43
Higginson, Thomas Wentworth   43, 59–60, 61–63, 69–70, 79, 91, 97
Hitchcock, Edward   25–26, 27, 31–33
Hitchcock, Orra White   31
Hofmann, Mark   94
Holland, Dr. Josiah Gilbert   55, 84
Holland, Elizabeth   55, 83
Holland, Sophia   28
Homestead   6, 7, 18, 48, 57, 64, 74, 77, 78, 86, 92
*Indicator, The*   45
Jackson, Helen Hunt   63, 77, 78, 79–81
Jackson, William   79, 81
*Jane Eyre*   39
Jantz, Richard   96
Judah, Theodore   52
Kerouac, Jack   13
Koch, Robert   22, 23
*Loaded Gun: Life and Death and Dickinson*   93
Longfellow, Henry Wadsworth   39
Lord, Otis Philips   78, 84
Lyon, Mary   35, 36–37
Lyric poetry   12
Marten, Benjamin   22
Massachusetts Agricultural College   68, 69

Merrill, Harriet  29
Monson, Massachusetts  16
Mount Holyoke  35–37, 54, 93
Newton, Benjamin Franklin  37–38
Nicholls, Arthur Bell  89
Norcross, Betsy Fay (grandmother)  16
Norcross, Francis  57, 68, 85
Norcross, Joel (grandfather)  16
Norcross, Lavinia (aunt)  18, 28, 57
Norcross, Lavinia (cousin)  28
Norcross, Louisa  57, 68, 85
*Odyssey, The*  11
Parker, Theodore  61
Phillips, Wendell  61
Poe, Edgar Allan  12, 43
Price, Hiram  81
Pullman, George  52
Root, Abiah Palmer  28–29, 36, 37
Ruskin, John  66
Saintine, X. B.  39
Synder, Gary  13
Sonnet  12–13
*Springfield Daily Republican*  55, 56, 58
Standing Bear, Chief  79, 81
Stephenson, George  51
Stone, Lucy  63
Stowe, Harriet Beecher  56, 80
Sweetser, Joseph  49
Thoreau, Henry David  43
Todd, Mabel Loomis  63, 84–85, 91, 92
Tracy, Sarah  28–29
Transcendentalism  7, 38, 41–43, 63
Tuberculosis  20, 21–23, 41, 79, 87
Tubman, Harriet  62
Underground Railroad  42
Unitarian Church  41
University of Massachusetts at Amherst  68
Upham, Thomas Cogswell  26
Valentine's Day  45–46
Wadsworth, Rev. Charles  47–48, 57, 84, 97
Watts, Isaac  58
West Center District School  19
West Street  19
Whitman, Walt  43
Whitney, Asa  51
Williams, Henry Willard  67–68
Wood, Abby  28–29